## 200 HA

Welcome to the luxurious premises of
the exclusive Hunter Clinic, world renowned
in plastic and reconstructive surgery,
set right on Harley Street, the centre of
elite clinical excellence, in the heart of
London's glittering West End!

Owned by two very different brothers,
Leo and Ethan Hunter, the Hunter Clinic
undertakes both cosmetic and reconstructive
surgery. Playboy Leo handles the rich and
famous clients, enjoying the red carpet
glamour of London's A-list social scene,
while brooding ex-army doc Ethan
focuses his time on his passion—
transforming the lives of injured war heroes
and civilian casualties of war.

Emotion and drama abound against the
backdrop of one of Europe's most glamorous
cities, as Leo and Ethan work
through their tensions and find women
who will change their lives for ever!

### 200 HARLEY STREET

*Glamour, intensity, desire—the lives and loves
of London's hottest team of surgeons!*

**Dear Reader**

It seems I've been doing a lot of continuities lately, and I seem to have made a bit of a speciality out of writing the final book in the series. Some people think it's difficult to pull off, but I kind of like it. I like it when the two main continuity characters finally get together after the tease of eight or so books, after I've been emotionally invested in their slow-burn relationship. I think, as readers, these are often the characters we most want to see get together. So giving them a happy-ever-after is always kind of special.

Giving Ethan and Olivia their HEA was even more so!

Many years ago, when I lived in the UK, I made a special trip to Harley Street. I even have a picture of the street sign, because it's one of those famous London Streets that everyone has heard of—like Fleet Street, Oxford Street or Park Lane. And it was exciting to be able to immerse myself in that world of top-notch, upper-class medical facilities again through the power of the written word. A world that, because I'd walked Harley Street, I felt I knew a little bit about.

It was especially fun to be working with seven other amazing authors to create such wonderful stories that overlapped and intertwined and are so much the stronger for all our individual voices. I felt, as the stories progressed, that we'd all been hanging out at Drake's together and I couldn't think of a better crowd to drink British ale with!

I hope you enjoy the final book in the *200 Harley Street* series. It was an absolute pleasure to write!

Love

*Amy*

**Recent titles by Amy Andrews:**

GOLD COAST ANGELS: HOW TO RESIST TEMPTATION†
ONE NIGHT SHE WOULD NEVER FORGET
SYDNEY HARBOUR HOSPITAL: EVIE'S BOMBSHELL*
HOW TO MEND A BROKEN HEART
SYDNEY HARBOUR HOSPITAL: LUCA'S BAD GIRL*
WAKING UP WITH DR OFF-LIMITS
JUST ONE LAST NIGHT…
RESCUED BY THE DREAMY DOC
VALENTINO'S PREGNANCY BOMBSHELL
ALESSANDRO AND THE CHEERY NANNY

*Sydney Harbour Hospital
†Gold Coast Angels

**These books are also available in eBook format
from www.millsandboon.co.uk**

# 200 HARLEY STREET: THE TORTURED HERO

BY
AMY ANDREWS

All rights reserved including the right of reproduction in whole or in part in any form. This edition is published by arrangement with Harlequin Books S.A.

This is a work of fiction. Names, characters, places, locations and incidents are purely fictional and bear no relationship to any real life individuals, living or dead, or to any actual places, business establishments, locations, events or incidents. Any resemblance is entirely coincidental.

This book is sold subject to the condition that it shall not, by way of trade or otherwise, be lent, resold, hired out or otherwise circulated without the prior consent of the publisher in any form of binding or cover other than that in which it is published and without a similar condition including this condition being imposed on the subsequent purchaser.

® and TM are trademarks owned and used by the trademark owner and/or its licensee. Trademarks marked with ® are registered with the United Kingdom Patent Office and/or the Office for Harmonisation in the Internal Market and in other countries.

First published in Great Britain 2014
by Mills & Boon, an imprint of Harlequin (UK) Limited,
Large Print edition 2015
Eton House, 18-24 Paradise Road,
Richmond, Surrey, TW9 1SR

© 2014 Harlequin Books S.A.

Special thanks and acknowledgement are given to Amy Andrews for her contribution to the *200 Harley Street* series

ISBN: 978-0-263-25451-8

Harlequin (UK) Limited's policy is to use papers that are natural, renewable and recyclable products and made from wood grown in sustainable forests. The logging and manufacturing processes conform to the legal environmental regulations of the country of origin.

Printed and bound in Great Britain
by CPI Antony Rowe, Chippenham, Wiltshire

**Amy Andrews** has always loved writing, and still can't quite believe that she gets to do it for a living. Creating wonderful heroines and gorgeous heroes and telling their stories is an amazing way to pass the day. Sometimes they don't always act as she'd like them to—but then neither do her kids, so she's kind of used to it. Amy lives in the very beautiful Samford Valley, with her husband and aforementioned children, along with six brown chooks and two black dogs.

She loves to hear from her readers. Drop her a line at www.amyandrews.com.au

## Dedication

For Carol, Scarlet, Alison, Lynne, Kate, Annie and Louisa.

It was fun working with you ladies— let's do it again sometime!

# 200 HARLEY STREET

*Glamour, intensity, desire—the lives and loves of
London's hottest team of surgeons!*

**For the next four months enter the world of London's
elite surgeons as they transform the lives of their patients
and find love amidst a sea of passions and tensions…!**

Renowned plastic surgeon and legendary playboy
Leo Hunter can't resist the challenge of unbuttoning
the intriguing new head nurse, Lizzie Birch!
***200 HARLEY STREET: SURGEON IN A TUX***
*by Carol Marinelli*

Glamorous Head of PR Lexi Robbins is determined
to make gruff, grieving and super-sexy Scottish surgeon Iain MacKenzie
her Hunter Clinic star!
***200 HARLEY STREET: GIRL FROM THE RED CARPET***
*by Scarlet Wilson*

Top-notch surgeons and estranged spouses
Rafael and Abbie de Luca find being forced to work together again
tough as their passion is as incendiary as ever!
***200 HARLEY STREET: THE PROUD ITALIAN***
*by Alison Roberts*

One night with his new colleague, surgeon Grace Turner, sees
former Hollywood plastic surgeon Mitchell Cooper daring to live again…
***200 HARLEY STREET: AMERICAN SURGEON IN LONDON***
*by Lynne Marshall*

Injured war hero Prince Marco meets physical therapist
Becca Anderson—the woman he once shared a magical *forbidden*
summer romance with long ago…
***200 HARLEY STREET: THE SOLDIER PRINCE***
*by Kate Hardy*

When genius micro-surgeon Edward North meets single mum
Nurse Charlotte King she opens his eyes to a whole new world…
***200 HARLEY STREET: THE ENIGMATIC SURGEON***
*by Annie Claydon*

Junior surgeon Kara must work with hot-shot
Irish surgeon Declan Underwood—the man she kissed at the hospital ball!
***200 HARLEY STREET: THE SHAMELESS MAVERICK***
*by Louisa George*

Brilliant charity surgeon Olivia Fairchild faces the man who once
broke her heart—damaged ex-soldier Ethan Hunter. Yet she's unprepared
for his haunted eyes and the shock of his sensual touch…!
***200 HARLEY STREET: THE TORTURED HERO** by Amy Andrews*

**Experience glamour, tension, heartbreak and emotion
at 200 HARLEY STREET
in this new eight-book continuity
from Mills & Boon® Medical Romance™**

**These books are also available in eBook format
and in two 200 HARLEY STREET collection bundles
from www.millsandboon.co.uk**

# CHAPTER ONE

ETHAN HUNTER NEEDED a drink.

*Bad.*

After five hours of complicated surgery his legs ached like a bitch and finding the bottom of a bottle was the only sure-fire way to soothe the fiery path of hot talons tearing from thigh to calf.

It was that or painkillers, and Ethan refused to be dependent on drugs.

'We're heading to Drake's, Ethan,' a voice with a thick Scottish brogue said from behind. 'Why don't you join us?'

A sudden silence descended into the male change-room as Ethan turned around to find Jock, the anaesthetist from the surgery, addressing him. He looked around at the four others, who'd all been chatting merrily until now. Clearly none of them were keen on having Ethan join them.

Jock didn't look particularly enthused either.

Not that he could blame them. The longer the surgery had taken, the more his legs had ached, and the more tense and terse he'd become. Accidentally dropping an instrument had been the last straw, and kicking it childishly across the floor until it clanged against the metallic kickboard of the opposite wall hadn't exactly been his most professional moment.

He hated prima donna surgeons, but his simmering frustration at his shot concentration *and* the pain had bubbled over at that point.

Even so, he didn't need or want their *duty* invitation, no matter how much he craved some alcoholic fortification. Ethan was just fine with drinking alone.

In fact, he preferred it.

'No thanks, Jock,' he said. 'I've got to get back to the clinic.'

Which was true. There was an important case file he needed to familiarise himself with on Leo's desk. And some classy fine malt whisky to go with it.

He looked around at his colleagues. 'Thanks for your help in there, everyone. Good job.'

There was a general murmuring of goodnights and then Ethan was alone. He sank gratefully onto the bench seat just behind him, easing his legs, muscles screaming, out in front of him. He shut his eyes as the pain lessened considerably and sat there for long minutes as the rush of relief anaesthetised the lingering tension in the rest of his body.

It felt so damn good to be off them!

But he couldn't sit here forever. Work called. He reluctantly opened his eyes and reached for his clothes.

The black cab pulled up in front of the imposing white Victorian facade on Harley Street. Like the many clinics and physician's offices that called Harley Street home, the Hunter Clinic was as exclusive as the address implied.

Ethan's father, celebrated plastic surgeon James Hunter, had founded it over three decades ago, and it had gone on to become world-renowned as much for its humanitarian and charity work with civilian and military casualties of war as for its A-list clients.

Thanks largely to his brother Leo.

Certainly not thanks to their father and the scandal that had not only resulted in his premature death through a heart attack but had almost caused the closure of the clinic over a decade ago.

Again, thanks to Leo's drive and commitment, it had been avoided.

Not that Ethan gave a rat's about any of that right at this moment. Thinking about his father and his previously rocky relationship with his brother always got things churned up inside, and tonight he was barely coping with standing upright.

Ethan paid the driver and hauled himself out of the back through sheer willpower alone. The only thing that kept him putting one foot in front of the other was the lure of Leo's whisky.

Ethan grimaced as he limped through the corridors to his brother's office, holding on to the polished wooden handrails for added support. His badly mangled ankle and knee felt ready to give at any second, and the effort it took for his muscles to support them was bringing him out in a sweat.

Ethan wished he hadn't neglected his physio so much, or ignored Lizzie—Leo's wife and his ex-home visit nurse—when she'd scolded him about not using his stick. He hated the damn stick, and the questions it inevitably aroused, and he didn't have time in his busy schedule for the intensive physio required—but at this moment in time he was prepared to embrace both.

Not that it would help him now.

But what *would* help beckoned just beyond Leo's door, and Ethan had never been so glad to get to his brother's office. It had once belonged to his father, and he'd used to hate being summoned here by the *great man* himself, in a rage over some imagined slight or other, as his father had slowly spiralled downwards into alcoholic depression.

Thankfully those days were gone, but it was pleasing to know that a decanter of finest whisky could still be found within the walls of this office—even if it was rarely touched.

The last ten paces to the bookshelves behind Leo's desk were agony, but ultimately worth it as Ethan wrapped his hand around the satisfyingly full decanter. He splashed two fingers of amber liquid into a glass tumbler that sat nearby and threw it straight back.

Searing heat hit the back of his throat and almost instantly tentacles of warmth unfurled outwards from his belly. He poured himself another one and threw that back too, enjoying how the spread of heat pushed back the relentless creep of pain.

A third glass was poured, but before Ethan drank it he picked up both it and the decanter in one hand and reached for the back of the plush leather swivel chair with the other. Leaning heavily against the solid piece of furniture, he dragged it towards him, thankful for the wheels that made it easier, throwing himself down into it, groaning as the weight came off his legs.

He shut his eyes on a deep sigh as screamingly tense muscles found release. Nursing his drink and the decanter against his chest, he flopped his head back into the cushiony leather headrest, tilted the chair backwards and swivelled gently from side to side, enjoying the rush from the twin sensations of heat and relief.

Ethan wasn't sure how long he sat there, idly twisting from side to side, his eyes shut, his tired muscles almost jelly now they'd been given permission to relax. He just knew it felt good to be non-weight-bearing.

Bliss. Ecstasy. Paradise.

But he *was* here for a reason—apart from the damn good whisky. He dragged his eyes open, knowing he couldn't put it off any longer. Finally acknowledging that was exactly what he *was* doing.

On Leo's desk there was a chart. The chart of a child with a terribly disfiguring condition that Ethan could help.

He could change little Ama's life.

He *would* change her life.

But Ama's case was complicated in more ways than one. Her condition was complex and would require multiple surgeries to correct.

But that wasn't the issue. Ethan thrived on complex.

It was the strings attached to the case that were the problem. Big, fat strings involving someone from his past and the unholy mess he'd made in his selfish, juvenile need to hurt his brother.

*Olivia Fairchild.*

Olivia's charity Fair Go was sponsoring Ama and her mother and an interpreter to travel from sub-Sahara Africa to London and the Hunter Clinic, for surgery and rehabilitation.

And she would be here—tomorrow.

Olivia who'd loved him. And he'd thrown it in her face by using her to get back at Leo. Flaunting her in front of his brother, knowing how much Leo had fallen for her, taunting him with the woman he couldn't have.

Olivia had been heartbroken when she'd realised. The look in her eyes that terrible, fateful day… He shuddered thinking about it now. The huge row he and Leo had got into, not knowing Olivia was listening to every ugly word. Him admitting that he was only interested in the sexy Aussie doc because Leo wanted her for himself.

It hadn't been true—not really. At the beginning, maybe, but not at that point. He'd enjoyed her company and there'd been something about her that had made him forget all his *stuff* when he was in her arms. The darkness that had been with him from his teenage years. The anguish over his mother's premature death. His dysfunctional relationship with his father. All had been lifted whenever she'd held him close.

But the damage had been done and his betrayal, his hurting her, had been unforgivable. *Toxic.* That was the word she'd used to describe his and Leo's relationship just before she'd fled back to Australia. And she'd been right. It had been toxic. And a lot of that had been on him.

But it wasn't any longer.

He'd been so angry and self-destructive back then. Angry at his mother for dying and the ensuing scandal over her infidelities, angry at his father for being weak and taking the easy, boozy way out after Francesca's death, and angrier at Leo for playing protector.

Protecting James from himself instead of confronting him over the inept drunk he'd become. And protecting Ethan from his father's wildly fluctuating mental state—from deep depression to manic rage—denying Ethan the opportunity to vent all his anger, frustration and loss.

Ethan cringed as he thought about what a bastard he'd been. He'd taken what he'd wanted with no regard for Olivia's feelings. Just stringing her along, thumbing his nose at her love, knowing how much Leo had had to grit his teeth every time he'd seen them together.

He'd thought himself so far above love back then—that he was immune to it. What a fool! It had taken a small, fierce, passionate firecracker of a woman from a foreign war-torn land to teach him how wrong he'd been. Maybe that was his punishment for Olivia?

Learning what love really meant and having it cruelly snatched away.

Ethan took a deep swallow of his drink, beating back memories of Aaliyah. He didn't need *that* guilt on top of his Olivia guilt tonight.

*No whisky bottle would be safe.*

Olivia…

Had she forgiven him? Did he even deserve her forgiveness?

He hoped so.

Or at least that they could put the past behind them. Because not only would he be seeing her tomorrow but he'd be working with her too. As a paediatric reconstructive surgeon, Olivia had been given clearance by Leo not only to assist in Ama's surgeries but to scrub in on any of the Hunter Clinic's cases during her stay in London.

The humanitarian side of the clinic, which was Ethan's baby, worked with charities from all round the world—Olivia's charity being just one. Consequently it had a reasonably robust operating schedule—many of the cases were kids. There would be plenty of opportunities for Olivia to keep her skills up to date while she juggled her hosting responsibilities for Ama.

And Ethan knew having another pair of hands—skilled hands—would allow them to do so much more.

*But team work was critical.*

He couldn't change what had happened in the past, and he was pretty damn sure she wouldn't want to rehash it either, but he could treat her with the respect she deserved going forward.

He took another sip of his whisky as the questions circled round and round his brain. Questions he didn't have answers for. Questions that could drive him nuts.

That could drive him to the bottom of Leo's decanter.

But he'd come too close to being his father, to taking the easy way out, a while back—he wasn't going there again.

He sighed and reached for the heavy walnut desk, grabbing hold and dragging the chair closer, trying to use his legs as little as possible. And there it was, right on the edge in the middle of the desk, Ama's chart.

Ethan placed the decanter and his glass on the table and pushed all thoughts of Olivia aside as he opened the chart and started to read.

Olivia Fairchild was late. She checked her watch for the hundredth time as she paid the taxi driver. The cool October evening, a far cry from the heat of Africa, closed in around her as the taxi took off and she turned to face the familiar building on Harley Street.

Late or not, she took a moment to collect herself and clear her throat of the emotion that she'd been battling on the cab-ride. She blinked back stupid tears. Getting Ama and her mother settled into their room at the Lighthouse Children's Hospital had been more emotional than she'd expected. She felt flustered and off-kilter rather than cool and professional, which was what she'd hoped to be when she came face to face with her past.

But Ama had got to her tonight—just as she had from day one. She'd been so apprehensive of her strange new world, and so distressed when her mother had left the room with the interpreter to attend to some paperwork, that Olivia had felt completely out of her depth.

For nine years Ama had known nothing other than a small village in sub-Sahara Africa where she'd been closeted away, not allowed to go to school or play with the other kids because of her disfiguring condition.

London must be terrifying.

Olivia, who had spent a lot of the past six weeks building a rapport with Ama, had tried her best to comfort the girl, but sometimes only mother-love would do and Ama had cried and cried until her mother returned.

And, oh, the way she'd clung had been gut-wrenching!

Olivia had been able to feel the frantic beat of Ama's heart through her painfully skinny ribs as the little girl had held onto her for dear life. And Olivia had clung right back, rocking her slightly, shushing her gently, feeling so inadequate in the face of the girl's anguish.

It had reminded her of the day she'd found Ama and her mother, both wailing and crying in the street, clinging to each other as two men engaged in a heated discussion had grabbed at them, trying to pull them apart. She hadn't been able to bear it.

A passing car hooted, bringing her back to the here and now, and Olivia shivered as the Hunter Clinic came back into focus. She took a deep breath, steeling herself to enter.

Her heart pounded as she mounted the stairs and pushed through the heavy doors. After-hours the clinic was hushed and deserted and she took a moment to absorb it all. Except for the stark whiteness of the updated décor, visible even in the darkened interior, it looked the same as she remembered—exclusive, luxurious, old money. It smelled the same. It *felt* the same.

And yet it didn't. It was familiar…yet not.

Maybe it was because *she* was different? Not the same starry-eyed Olivia who had trusted her heart to the Hunter boys only to be used in their toxic games and have it crushed into the dirt.

Older. Wiser.

*Stronger.*

It was warm inside and she undid the toggles on her duffle coat as her boot heels tapped on the exquisite grey and black marble floor on her way to Leo's office. It felt like a lifetime ago now since she'd walked these corridors on her frequent trips to see Ethan.

*Ethan.*

Olivia's heart skipped a beat as her stride faltered.

No. She would not think about him tonight. She wasn't here to see Ethan. She was here to see Leo.

Ethan would come tomorrow. And tomorrow would be soon enough.

Despite only the most subdued light, coming from lamps placed in discreet alcoves, her feet took her to Leo's office without any real direction from her brain. Once there she didn't stop to give herself time to think or doubt, she just reached up to knock on the door, surprised when it swung silently open under the weight of her closed hand.

For a moment, peering into the sumptuous darkened office, with just a desk lamp illuminating the room, she thought the man sitting at the desk, head bent over a chart, looked like Leo and she smiled.

'Leo,' she called from the doorway, her voice hushed as seemed appropriate in the quietness of the deserted building.

Ethan, who'd been too intent to register the knock, looked up as his brother's name spilled from Olivia's lips, and even a decade down the track he still felt the impact of that mouth.

Wide and sexy, forming a natural pout that had always fascinated him. A mouth he'd kissed.

He'd *missed*.

It was a startling realisation for a man who'd

felt dead inside for the past year. And he wasn't sure he liked it.

What the hell was she doing here? Didn't her flight arrive early tomorrow morning?

'Olivia,' he acknowledged, watching as her eyes, always two huge chocolate pools shimmering with emotional intensity, grew even rounder.

He should stand—innate good manners dictated that he should—but his legs felt about as supportive as wet noodles and he didn't trust them. Thankfully Olivia seemed too stunned to call him on it.

Olivia blinked as all the oxygen in the room was sucked right out. 'Oh...'

*Ethan.* Not Leo. *Ethan.* Her heart pounded in time to the drumming of his name through her brain.

*Ethan. Ethan. Ethan.*

'I'm sorry, I know I'm late, but...' She nervously checked her watch. 'I'm supposed to be meeting Leo here.'

Ethan hadn't been sure what they'd say to each other when he and Olivia came face to face again. They'd spoken twice on the phone about the case, which had been brisk and professional, but he'd thought it would be different when they were looking at each other. That old hurts might have fizzled out.

Evidently not, judging by the wariness in Olivia's startled gaze.

Her first words were not warm and welcoming. There was no *let bygones be bygones* about her demeanour. She hadn't smiled for *him* as she had when she'd mistaken him for Leo. And, perversely, it bugged him.

There was a wariness, a distance in her gaze. As if they were strangers instead of ex-lovers. And a part of him wanted to snatch her up, taste that pouty mouth again, remind her how good they'd been together.

*If only he could get up without falling flat on his face!*

'He's at home,' Ethan said abruptly, angry at the direction of his thoughts.

For God's sake, he was lucky she hadn't slapped him in the face. Clearly he wasn't thinking straight. *Clearly* he was just too damn tired to be facing ghosts tonight.

Olivia frowned. 'Oh...'

But...she'd called Leo the moment they'd landed and they'd arranged it. She delved around inside her bag for her mobile phone, pulling it out. Immediately she noticed two missed calls and a text—all from Leo.

*Apologies. Something came up. Get Ethan up to speed and you can catch me up tomorrow.*

'Something came up,' Olivia said, looking from the phone to Ethan as she relayed the text.

Ethan grunted as a rather unpleasant thought occurred to him. Leo had texted him during surgery, asking him to familiarise himself with Ama's chart—*on his desk*—before the morning. Had Leo set this up so he and Olivia could get their first meeting over and done with in private—to give them room and privacy to clear the air?

His relationship with his brother was the best it

had been in years, but he didn't appreciate being manipulated like this.

'I bet it did,' Ethan said dryly.

Olivia put her phone back in her bag. 'He wants me to get you up to speed.'

Ethan had sometimes forgotten, just looking at her, that Olivia was Australian. Her flawless peaches and cream complexion seemed eminently English, and it was only when she opened her mouth and the flat Aussie drawl came out that he remembered. That and the opal ring she still wore on the middle finger of her right hand—a gift from her parents for her eighteenth birthday.

'No time like the present,' he agreed grimly.

If Leo *had* set them up then it would be foolish not to use the time wisely.

'Come in.' He gestured, suddenly realising she was still standing just inside the doorframe. 'Take a seat.' He indicated with his head for her to take the one on the other side of Leo's desk.

Her movements seemed awkward and unsure as she drew closer. She certainly didn't seem to be in any hurry to reach her destination, and he waited impatiently for her to take her seat, his gaze drifting to the way the denim of her jeans clung to legs still as slender as he remembered.

As she drew level his gaze moved up. Her red turtle-necked skivvy was mostly hidden by the thick navy jacket she was wearing, but it did emphasise the length of her neck to perfection. A neck he'd explored in intimate detail.

Olivia was conscious of his gaze on her as she moved into the room. Heat flared in her belly as she remembered the way he used to look at her—all intensity and wicked, wicked purpose.

*Before he broke her heart.*

She was thankful for the thick wool of her coat hiding nipples suddenly taking on a mind of their own.

She didn't have time for recalcitrant nipples.

They were two professionals, working together for the good of a patient. Yes, they had history, but if they kept things collegial, if they kept their focus on Ama, they'd be fine.

She was here to do a job and then get the hell out of Dodge.

She'd been burned by this man before. And fire had already claimed too much of what she'd loved.

Olivia sat, glancing briefly around at Leo's office. It didn't appear to have changed much since the days when it had belonged to his father. All dark and masculine—a stark contrast to the bright modern white outside.

Her gaze returned to Ethan and for long moments they just looked at each other. His lids were half shuttered; his gaze was totally guarded. He looked so...*distant* and she shivered.

He picked up the nearby whisky decanter and splashed some into a glass, silently asking her with a raising of his eyebrow if she wanted any. She shook her head, surprised to see him drinking, knowing how much he'd despised his father for his weakness where the amber liquid was concerned.

*Keep it professional, Liv.*

'You've changed,' she blurted out.

And it was nothing to do with the drinking.

Ethan's eyes were the same deep brown as hers, but he had those amazing golden flecks in them that used to *glow* with fire and passion. He'd been so angry back then that they'd flashed and flared all the time as he'd struggled with his demons—his father's alcoholism, his mother's death and what he'd perceived as his brother's molly-coddling.

But she'd also seen them glow and flash at other times too. At work when he was totally absorbed in a surgery. And in bed…

There was no glow tonight. Just a dull glimpse of what had been. It was as if it had been snuffed out. Suffocated.

What had happened to turn those gorgeous flashing eyes so damn bleak? And his perfect chiselled face so damn gaunt? His severe hair-cut didn't help. Nor did the weary lines around his eyes. Not to mention that he needed a shave. His shaggy regrowth looked more salt than pepper at the grand old age of thirty-five.

Was he suffering some kind of PTSD from being blown half to hell during his last tour?

'You haven't,' he said, interrupting her reverie.

It was Olivia's turned to snort. 'Yes, I have.'

She'd been through more than her fair share of heartbreak these past ten years, and although she'd come through it stronger it had changed her utterly.

Ethan paused slightly, then acknowledged the truth of it with a nod. She was right. She was more reserved, less carefree. Her gaze was not as open, was more...*distant.*

Had that been his unforgivable actions or just getting older? Life in general?

Or had something else caused the coolness in her eyes?

'I just don't need to resort to whisky to prove it.'

Ethan felt the accusation hit him in the chest with all the power of a sledgehammer.

He threw back the contents of the glass and slammed it down on the desktop. 'It's been a long day, Olivia,' he said, his jaw so tight it felt as if it was going to crumble from the pressure. 'Surgery is over and I'm off duty. A few glasses of Scotland's best isn't going to hurt.'

Olivia had never been one to beat around the

bush and she wasn't about to start now. Clearly something was eating at Ethan—something had snuffed out the light. And, whilst she might not know what it was, she sure as hell knew whisky wasn't the answer.

'I'm sure that's exactly how your father started out.'

# CHAPTER TWO

ETHAN'S HEART POUNDED a furious tattoo in his chest. Having his father shoved in his face was always a red rag to a bull, but pure overproof rage surged through his system at her matter-of-fact taunt. If anyone knew the location of his soft underbelly it was Olivia. And she'd never been afraid to call him on his crap.

It was the *Australian way*, she'd assured him all those years ago.

He gripped the edge of the desk and lurched to his feet, too angry even to register the limp protest of gelatinous muscles. 'Go to hell, Olivia,' he snapped.

Her words stung. They stung hard. Because they'd found their mark so accurately. After he'd been discharged from the hospital in Germany and returned to the UK to recuperate from his injuries he *had* drunk way too much.

Trying to block out the pain and the dreams and the guilt.

Leo's email had saved him. The offer to come back to the clinic and head up its humanitarian programme had been just the right bait to wave in front of him and he'd reached for it like a drowning man, knowing that he was treading the same slippery slope his father had trod before he'd slipped away altogether.

But he wasn't that guy any more. And it infuriated him to be pigeonholed after a few minutes' reacquaintance.

*She had no freaking idea what he'd been through.*

Olivia stood too, refusing to have him standing over her, trying to intimidate her with his height and breadth and sheer masculine presence—which he still had in spades despite his more mature looks.

So, she'd annoyed him—*good*!

Maybe it would make him realise that sitting alone in an office at nine o'clock at night with a decanter full of whisky wasn't the answer to whatever was eating him.

'I'll follow you down, shall I?' she enquired calmly.

Ethan pressed his closed fists into the hard wood of the desktop and prayed for patience. He didn't need her judgement—he could do that plenty on his own.

'I think you can bring me up to speed in the morning,' he said through clenched teeth. He was too tired for this crap. 'I'm going home. See yourself out.'

At least going home was his plan, but by the time he'd taken a few paces the adrenaline from his surge of anger had worn off and the message from his quad muscles that they were too fatigued to hold him upright had finally broken through the righteous indignation swamping his brain.

His legs buckled.

Olivia leapt forward in alarm as Ethan wobbled and then toppled sideways, reaching out for the desk wildly in an attempt to stop himself from falling on his butt. She grabbed hold of his arm and between her and the desk they saved him from being a rather inelegant crumpled heap on the expensive Turkish rug.

'What the hell, Ethan?' she said as he leaned heavily against her, struggling for balance. 'How much *have* you had to drink?' she asked.

Ethan sucked air in and out between his teeth as his muscles protested. 'Not the booze,' he choked out, one hand reaching for a screaming thigh muscle. 'It's my damn legs.'

Olivia believed him. He definitely wasn't drunk. His words weren't slurred and he didn't stink of alcohol. In fact, with her nose damn near the vicinity of his throat, she could say for sure that he smelled the way he always had—of utter hedonism. Total crack for the olfactory system. It swamped over her now in a sweet pheromone cloud, and her body responded accordingly.

Honestly, the man was waging chemical warfare on her body and he didn't even know it, thanks to whatever was going on with his legs.

'Here, come on,' she said, staggering under the weight of him a little as she slung his arm over her shoulder. 'Over to the lounge.'

Ethan didn't have much of a choice. His thighs

were trembling now from the effort of just standing and he felt as weak as a kitten. She led and
he followed, and he felt about as potent and
virile as a postage stamp.

'I'm fine,' he said as soon as they were near
enough to the couch to reach for it. 'Let go.'

Olivia eased away as he flopped down onto the
firm leather of the elegant Chesterfield and gave
a relieved groan, his hands automatically reaching for his thigh muscles, his eyes shutting, his
head flopping back as he kneaded up and down
their length. She knelt down in front of him, his
knees either side of her shoulders, resting back
on her haunches, and waited for him to recover.

It took a few minutes for the creases in his face
to start to iron out a little. 'What happened?' she
asked quietly.

His hands stopped their massaging briefly before starting up again.

'Is it from when you were injured during your
last tour?' she prompted, when it didn't look as
if he was about to answer her any time soon.

His eyes flicked open and Olivia was struck

again by how dull and lifeless they looked. No spark. No glitter.

'How did you know?'

She gave him a half-smile, trying to lighten the mood. 'We *do* have newspapers in Australia, you know. And this new-fangled thing called the worldwide web—which, you know, even goes all the way to Australia.' Her smile died on her lips when it was apparent he wasn't going to join her. 'You'll be amazed at what you can find on it,' she murmured.

Ethan pulled his head off the cushioned comfort of the lounge and pierced her with his gaze. Her honey-brown hair fell in wavy disorder around her face and he remembered vividly how it had felt spread out across his chest.

'You kept tabs on me?'

Olivia sucked in a breath as his low, gravelly voice swept hot fingers along the muscles deep inside her. And was that a flare bursting to life in those golden flecks?

'No,' she said, annoyed that even tired and in pain he could think such a thing.

*Clearly his ego hadn't been injured.*

'I haven't spent the past decade *pining* over you, Ethan Hunter, if that's what you think,' she clarified, her voice snippy even to her own ears. 'I researched the clinic online when I was looking at partnering with you guys. The newspaper articles about how you evacuated an entire hospital that was being heavily shelled showed up in the search.'

Ethan dropped his head back again and shut his eyes against the annoyance in hers and the echo of memories. He'd been meaning to check up on her over the years, but military life had been full-on and there'd always been an excuse not to.

And then he'd met Aaliyah.

Olivia watched him a little longer, the kneading of his long fingers hypnotic. Part of her wanted to take over—the Olivia of ten years ago would have.

This Olivia curled her hands into fists by her sides and said, 'What are your injuries?'

Ethan sighed, lifting his head off the lounge again. 'Legs shot to hell. Right knee and ankle torn up by shrapnel.'

'Have they been reconstructed?'

He nodded. 'As best they could. They're never going to be the same again, though.'

'Do you have some kind of physio regime, because your legs don't seem to be very strong. I'd have thought you'd need some kind of a walking aid—a stick or something?' She frowned, thinking back to the articles she'd read. 'It's been about a year, right?'

Ethan grunted. 'Yes,' he said tersely. 'And, yes, I have a regime.'

It took Olivia a second or two to realise she'd asked the wrong question. 'Do you *follow* it?' She folded her arms. 'Religiously?'

Ethan glared at her. God, she sounded like Lizzie. And Leo. And a lot of well-meaning other people who didn't have a freaking clue about the realities of his injuries.

'It's none of your damn business,' he growled.

'It *is* my damn business if you're going to collapse on the floor in the middle of operating on Ama.'

Ethan bristled at the implication, and at the un-flinching demand he saw in her eyes. She was calling him on his professionalism and leaving him in no doubt that she was holding him to account. It rankled. But still, it was preferable to the pity he usually saw reflected in other people's eyes.

The *poor you* look that got under his skin like an army of marching ants.

She didn't seem to give a damn about the fact of his injuries or even how he'd got them—just that he could do his job. She was being a doctor. And it was in equal parts satisfying and irritating

'I'm not going to be collapsing on anyone,' he snapped. 'I just stood for an extraordinary amount of time today.'

'Which shouldn't matter if you'd been diligent with your physio,' Olivia said.

She knew Ethan. She knew he wouldn't respond to her empathy. God knew, the empathy and protection Leo had tried to force upon him all those years ago had driven a huge wedge between the brothers and she'd been just one of the casualties.

She knew he wouldn't let her massage his legs

or talk about what had happened. But, having worked out in the field herself, in places no one should have to live, she did know that military men responded best to tough love.

'I've been a little busy trying to establish the humanitarian side of the clinic,' he snapped. 'I do what I can when I can.'

Olivia drummed her fingers against her biceps. 'Well, it looks like it's not enough. You should be stronger than this by now.'

Ethan knew she was right, but…it *had* been an unusual day. He let his head flop back again.

He needed to make time to get stronger in his legs. He'd gone from two months in hospital and multiple surgeries to home and feeling sorry for himself to throwing everything he had into his new role at the Hunter Clinic—none of which had been conducive to the hard yards he needed to do.

As Olivia watched he seemed to melt into the couch, exhaustion in every line of his body, and part of her wanted to lay her cheek on his nearby knee and just sit with him in silence. She was surprised to feel such tenderness for him after what had happened. But then the heat in her belly had been a surprise too, after all these years.

She nudged his knee with her shoulder. '*Have* you got a stick you should be using?'

Ethan lifted a hand off his thigh and massaged his forehead with it. He wished she'd just be quiet, already—she was like Jiminy freaking Cricket. 'Yes…' he said on a sigh.

'And the reason you don't appear to have it with you is…?'

Ethan lifted his head. 'I hate the damn thing,' he muttered.

Olivia raised an eyebrow. Did he realise how much he sounded like a petulant child? 'Does it affect your tough guy image, Ethan? I wouldn't have thought you so vain.'

Ethan snorted. Did she *really* think this was about vanity? 'No, it's just…' He shook his head, shut his eyes, rested his head back again as he realised he was about to admit the truth. 'It… invites conversations I just don't want to have.'

The heaviness in his voice reached right inside her gut and squeezed. *Hard.* She knew all too well how hard rehashing things could be—talking about stuff that sometimes you just didn't want to talk about. Especially with people who had no connection to you.

So many people had wanted to talk to her after what had happened to her parents, had wanted to reminisce, lament, vent. And she'd spent an awful lot of time avoiding them.

Without thinking about it she slid a hand onto his knee. The fine wool of his trousers was soft against her palm, the contours of his knee hard.

'Ethan…'

Ethan lifted his head again as her touch caused a riot of sensations up his aching leg. *Good* sensations. She was barely touching him at all, but still it felt as if she'd injected pop rocks into his thigh. He looked at her neat fingernails and remembered how good they'd felt on other parts of his body. How *good* they'd been together. How much they'd sizzled.

*How insatiable they'd been.*

His reasons for being with Olivia might not have been exactly altruistic, but they'd been amazingly compatible in the bedroom.

Which reminded him how long it had been since he'd been with a woman. A year.

Not since Aaliyah.

He dragged his eyes off her hand and looked up. Their gazes locked. The worst thing about her touch was how familiar it felt. Here in this clinic, with this woman from his past looking at him with patience and compassion, it would be so easy to grab hold and travel back to a time when he'd been able to lose himself in her and have everything else fade to black.

But it felt…disloyal. To Aaliyah. And he despised himself just a little bit more.

'Just go, Olivia.'

*Go before I kiss you. Before I haul you up on the couch beside me. Before I beg you to stay.*

*Before I use you one more time.*

Olivia's belly clenched at the flare of heat that fired Ethan's dull gaze. She'd seen that look before. She knew what it meant. She knew what he wanted. Her breath grew thick in her throat as things south of her waistband stirred and strained, demanding she respond in the most primal way.

His nostrils flared as the silence stretched between them and she could feel the coiled intensity of his muscles. He wanted her. She could see that. Hell, half an hour in his company and she wanted him too.

But, unlike last time, she wanted *all* of him. She wanted his story and his sadness and his shadows. And she wasn't going to settle for scraps. For some quick roll in the hay while he made love to her with dead eyes. Because having sex with Ethan had never been a one-time thing for her and she needed to protect herself better than last time.

She was here for Ama. And then she was leaving.

*She was not having sex with Ethan Hunter.*

Olivia pushed herself shakily to her feet. She was standing between his knees now and an image of her straddling him played in glorious Technicolor inside her head.

She took a step back. 'Are you—?' She cleared her throat of its sudden wobble. 'Are you heading home soon?'

Ethan shook his head. He probably hadn't been

very capable of standing prior to Olivia touching him; he for damn sure wasn't now. 'I'll sleep here tonight.'

Olivia nodded. It seemed best, considering walking had been a monumental effort. 'Are you…will you be okay?'

'Dandy,' he said sarcastically, annoyed at her distant propriety—a far cry from the heat of the look they'd just exchanged.

Olivia ignored his terseness. 'What time do you want to meet in the morning?' she asked.

'Be here at nine.' His tone was dismissive and he hoped she got the message—*get the hell out.*

Olivia got the message. It rankled, but she didn't want to get into anything more with him tonight. It seemed their incendiary attraction still simmered and she didn't trust that the line between angry and passionate wouldn't blur and they wouldn't do something they'd *both* regret in the morning.

She turned on her heel and headed towards the desk, where her bag had been dumped when Ethan had fallen. She reached for it, her gaze falling on the decanter of whisky. She snatched it up. It could leave with her as well.

Out of sight, out of mind.

'You don't have to take it,' he said derisively from behind her. 'Even if I was capable of hauling my butt off this couch, I'm done with drinking tonight.'

Olivia turned, slinging the straps of her handbag over her shoulder. 'Consider this as my way of delivering you from temptation.' And with that she headed for the door.

Ethan tracked her progress, her clinging jeans, the swish of her honey-brown hair down the back of her coat way too fascinating for his own peace of mind.

A surge of what felt like good old-fashioned lust swept through his system.

He didn't feel very delivered at all.


Ethan was woken by a hard shake to his shoulder who knew how many hours later? Except where there had been darkness there was now light. *Way too much light.*

Daylight streamed like glory from heaven

through the open slats of the dark wooden blinds dressing the window under which the chesterfield sat, piercing like needles into his eyeballs.

'Ugh,' he groaned, shutting his eyes tight. 'Somebody turn down the sun.'

'What the hell are you doing here?' Leo demanded, ignoring his brother's protests as he yanked up the blind, causing a tsunami of sunlight.

Ethan groaned louder. 'It was late,' he said, shielding his eyes. 'I crashed here.'

'I should start charging you rent,' Leo muttered.

Ethan cracked an eyelid open to find his brother lounging against the far arm of the couch. He squinted at his watch. It was six-thirty in the morning. 'Lizzie kick you out of bed?'

Leo grinned, which was way too much for Ethan at this hour of the morning. 'She's not sleeping very well,—has to keep getting up to go to the bathroom. I'm trying to give her as much room as possible.'

Ethan was pleased his brother had found love, but such happiness was a bit hard to take—especially hard on the heels of his less than stellar reunion with Olivia. He sat and swung his legs over the edge of the couch, pleased to feel the strength back in his quads.

'You look like hell,' Leo said cheerfully.

'Gee…thanks.' Compared to last night he felt like a million dollars.

'You going to head home or shower here?'

Ethan ran his hands through his hair. 'I'll use your bathroom.' He always kept spare clothes in his office, and a private bathroom was one of the perks of being the director—or related to him anyway.

Ethan owned the clinic jointly with his brother, but had gladly ceded control to him when he'd decided to leave everything tainted with the Hunter name behind and put his medical degree to good use in the army. Leo had been angry that he was skipping out on his family responsibilities, especially with the clinic in such trouble after his father's scandal, and had spent the next ten years trying to involve his younger brother in the day-to-day running of the clinic.

But Ethan hadn't cared. He'd not wanted any

part of lipo and boob jobs on a bunch of movie stars. He'd been doing *real* work and Leo could do whatever the hell he liked to salvage the professional and financial reputation of the once renowned Hunter Clinic.

And then he'd been blown all to hell and Leo had made him an offer he couldn't refuse. An offer he'd desperately needed to stop him from sliding into an abyss of self-pity.

Leo pushed up off the arm. 'When you're done I'll buy you breakfast.'

Three quarters of an hour later they were sitting inside a nearby café, tucking into a traditional English breakfast. They were both on their second cup of coffee.

'So. You saw Olivia last night, I take it?'

Ethan looked up from his plate. 'Yes. Nicely orchestrated,' he said with derision.

Completely unabashed, Leo said, 'How did that go?'

'How do you think it went?'

'Not as well as I'd hoped, by the sounds of it.'

'Let's just say I wasn't in the best shape when she arrived. She pretty much accused me of being one step away from the old man and then chewed my ear off about not doing my physio.'

Leo laughed. 'Still the same blunt old Olivia, huh?'

Ethan grunted, then took a sip of his coffee. 'She is and she isn't. There's a…reserve about her…she's not her usual vivacious self.'

'Maybe that's just being around you?'

Ethan contemplated his brother's observation. *Maybe it was.* 'Anyway…it didn't go well. She has your decanter of whisky too, by the way.'

Leo laughed harder. 'Did you discuss the case at all?'

Ethan shook his head. 'She's coming to your office at nine to brief us both.'

Leo quirked an eyebrow at his brother. 'Am I to be an intermediary?'

Ethan looked at his older brother. His tone was light but their history with Olivia Fairchild was complex. And, apart from one aborted attempt on the day of Leo's wedding, Ethan had never really apologised for his behaviour where that was concerned. He'd not only hurt Olivia but he'd also hurt Leo—deliberately.

Because he could.

He put his coffee cup down in its saucer. 'No. Of course not. About that...about Olivia...about what happened between all of us—'

'Don't worry about it,' Leo interrupted. 'Water under the bridge.'

'No.' Ethan shook his head. 'I was out of line.'

'Yes, you were.' Leo grinned. 'But...I knew deep down she never really liked me—not in that way. She certainly never gave me any reason to think there was anything other than friendship on her behalf. But...she was so gorgeous...my ego got in the way.'

*Gorgeous.* Yes, Leo was right. Olivia had been vivacious, sparkling, witty. Quick with a laugh and a snappy one-liner.

And utterly gorgeous.

'That doesn't make my behaviour any less reprehensible. You were right. I was using her to get at you and I'm sorry. I was pretty self-destructive there for a while, huh?'

Leo shrugged. 'Losing Mum was hard on you.'

'And not on you?'

'Ethan…we've made our peace. We *both* did things wrong and I don't expect you to spend the rest of your life apologising for something that happened a long time ago which we've put behind us.'

He paused and pierced his brother with a look that Ethan had come to know as his clinic director look.

'And I'm not the one you need to apologise to. That's what you were supposed to be doing last night.'

Ethan grimaced. 'Yeah. That didn't happen.' He glanced at his brother, who held his gaze with unwavering intensity. 'She refused to accept my apology last time. What makes you think she will now?'

'It's been a long time,' Leo said. 'And she's never struck me as being someone to hold a grudge.'

'It was pretty unforgivable.'

Leo nodded in agreement. 'You need to make it right, though. You'll be working with her again over the next few months. You have to clear the air.'

Ethan knew Leo was right. Once upon a time that would have rankled, as everything about his brother's authority and over-protectiveness had rankled. But he'd done a lot of growing up and recognised good advice when he heard it. 'I know.'

There was silence for the next few minutes as they finished their breakfast. Leo put his utensils down on his plate and looked at his brother. 'I thought you and her might…'

Ethan glanced up from his breakfast. The possibility of he and Olivia glimmered for a moment. Her touch on his leg last night was almost tangible again, the way they'd been together settling around him in a fine mist he could almost taste.

But then memories of another woman—a woman he'd loved, a woman he'd left to die—pushed into the possibilities, beating them back, drowning them in a tide of guilt.

*Aaliyah.*

Ethan threw his napkin on his plate. 'Let's go.'

# CHAPTER THREE

RUNNING EARLY THIS time, Olivia smiled at Leo as she walked into his office an hour later. She'd always had a soft spot for the incredibly hard-working elder Hunter brother and it hadn't been killed by time, distance or past wrongs. Yes, she'd told them their relationship was toxic but that hadn't really been Leo's fault.

Leo had been caught in the middle between his father and his brother and had practically killed himself to do right by both of them.

It was Ethan's bitterness that had been the true destructive force.

She thrust the whisky decanter she'd hauled all the way back in the taxi at him as she neared. 'I relieved Ethan of this last night.'

'Yes, he mentioned it.' Leo grinned taking it from her and then sweeping her into a huge hug.

'I can't believe it's been ten years,' he said as he pulled back. 'How have you been?'

Olivia gave her standard reply. 'Fine.' Because the truth was less than fine, and she refused to give it power over her. 'But now…what about you? Not only married but a baby on the way? I have to meet this girl!'

Easily deflected, Leo chatted for ten minutes about Lizzie and babies and their life together and Olivia was heartened to hear that Leo had found the happiness he'd always deserved. She'd valued and enjoyed his friendship and had been saddened by its becoming another casualty of Ethan's destructive streak.

If she'd only been smarter she would have chosen the older Hunter brother. But the heart wanted what the heart wanted, and from the moment she'd laid eyes on Ethan she'd been officially off the market!

She'd fallen hard for his good looks, charm and intelligence. Yes, he'd been angry, and hurting too, but he'd oozed undeniable potential from every cell in his being. She'd just known that one day he would do great things.

And that had been pretty damn irresistible.

But she would have resisted had she known she was going to cause an even bigger rift between the two brothers. She'd thought she'd be able to help them reconnect, to heal the cracks in their relationship that had been gutting to watch.

Her tender heart had been touched by the suffering they'd endured—their mother's death and the scandalous details of her life that had come to light after, and their father's messy slide into the bottle. Coming from a background that placed family above *everything*, she hadn't been able to bear the thought of what the Hunter boys must have been through growing up and she'd desperately wanted to help.

She'd wanted to show Ethan, and Leo by extension, how wonderful a loving relationship—like the one her parents had—could be. And to bring them back to each other.

But Ethan had been on a different page and she hadn't got the memo.

The light chatter stopped as soon as Ethan entered the room. Olivia was relieved to see him looking much more human this morning. Back to his usual level of *ooh la la* in a suit and tie. He'd hadn't shaved, but the lines around his eyes had disappeared. His gait was strong and sure even with the slight limp as he strode towards the desk.

She'd lain awake half the night thinking about their reunion and the state of his health. He seemed even more messed up than he had been a decade ago. Lucky for her, life had hardened her sappy little heart over the years, and the urge to fix Ethan Hunter had withered and died a long time ago. He was a big boy who could take care of himself.

Leo looked from one to the other as she and Ethan stood awkwardly in front of his desk. 'Let's get down to it, shall we?' he suggested.

'Yes,' they both said in unison, and then glanced guiltily at each other before simultaneously looking away.

Leo sighed. 'Take a seat,' he said, indicating the chairs opposite him, and Olivia wasn't sure whose butt was on whose respective chair faster—hers or Ethan's.

Clearly Ethan was keen to get this over with.

Good.

That made two of them.

Ethan strode into the Lighthouse Children's Hospital just prior to lunch. He'd walked from Harley Street. Last night the thought of walking any distance had been beyond him, but he usually walked from the clinic to the Lighthouse, and also to Princess Catherine's Hospital, time permitting.

The Hunter Clinic and its team of surgeons had operating privileges at both hospitals and neither was far to walk. Still, after Olivia's dressing-down last night he was using his stick, even if he did have plans to abandon it just prior to seeing his patients.

Olivia had accused him of vanity last night and he'd set her straight on that. Drawing attention to himself, to his injuries, wasn't something he was keen on. But it was more than that. A surgeon with a walking stick just sent the wrong kind of message. Especially in the world of plastics and reconstructive surgery. Patients wondered about a surgeon who couldn't heal himself.

Leaving his stick in one of the empty offices, he did his rounds. Being a visiting surgeon, he didn't have any junior doctors to accompany him but always made sure one of the nursing staff on each ward did. Nothing annoyed the nurses more than a doctor coming in and making changes to treatment and then leaving again without informing them.

And Ethan had learned a long time ago never to upset the nursing staff. That nurses were a vital part of the medical team—the interface between the doctor and the patient.

And you annoyed them at your own peril.

He prided himself on having good relationships with the nursing staff wherever he went, and at the Lighthouse particularly.

He left Ama to last. There was a lot that needed to be done before she went to Theatre next week and he wanted to have a clean plate today so he could focus solely on her. Plus Olivia was with her, and for some reason he was unaccountably nervous. It was obvious from her briefing this morning that this case was dear to her and he found himself not wanting to disappoint her.

He'd done that once already and was desperate to make amends.

He made his way to Ama's room by himself, assuring Ama's nurse, who was busy with another of her patients, that he would keep her up to date with the tests and procedures he was ordering. He heard laughter as he approached—Olivia's laughter. With her petite frame she looked as if she'd have one of those light and tinkly girly laughs, but it was surprisingly deep and throaty and it always came out at full roar—coming not just from her belly but from her heart.

He remembered it well from back when she used to smile at him, when she used to laugh.

It evoked powerful memories of a turbulent time in his life. A time when her laughter had helped ease a lot of his frustrations.

She had her back to the door when he pulled up and he lounged against the frame, observing her for long moments. She was sitting on the bed opposite a little girl who sat cross-legged in the lap of an older woman. Their skin was as dark and burnished as the finest ebony.

Ama and her mother, he assumed. Although

he could only see them in profile and therefore the defect, which he knew to be quite significant, wasn't showing, given that it was the other side of Ama's face. He also noted the colourful headscarf that Ama wore draped over her affected side, obscuring it completely.

Looked at from this vantage point, Ama looked perfectly normal. But he'd seen the pictures—NOMA had ravaged the right side of her face, leaving her terribly disfigured.

A chequerboard sat between them and they were engrossed in a lively game. A third person—a young woman with skin more of a mocha colouring—sat on a chair beside the bed, also involved, switching between English and an unfamiliar language and laughing as Ama made a run of the board.

'Ama, you are getting much too good at this,' Olivia said, and laughed that full throaty laugh again.

The woman in the chair spoke to Ama in what he presumed was her own language and the girl giggled, her eyes sparkling in absolute delight.

Ethan was struck by how intimate the cosy little circle appeared. They all seemed very comfortable in each other's company. Ama's mother was looking at Olivia as if she was some kind of saint and Ama was smiling so big at Olivia, her eyes sparkling so brightly, it was like the sun shining.

Olivia passed over a red chequer piece to Ama and Ama laughed again, the whites of her eyes flashing as she held on to Olivia's hand for long moments before accepting the spoils and crowning her victorious piece.

Ama said something in her own tongue and the woman Ethan assumed was the translator said, 'Ama thinks she's winning.'

Olivia laughed again, and even with the distance between them, it whispered against his skin.

'Oh, does she, now?' Olivia said with mock indignation. 'We'll see how easy it is for her to win when I'm tickling her,' she announced, raising her hands and wiggling her fingers in Ama's direction before launching a tickle attack on a giggling, squealing Ama.

The chequerboard was upended, but nobody seemed to mind as general pandemonium ensued.

Ethan was struck by the genuine connection between Olivia and Ama and her mother. There was nothing forced or stilted—just an easy familiarity. But there was also an unspoken trust in their byplay, and Ethan knew how hard Olivia would have had to work to gain that trust. To take them out of their own country, away from everything they knew and trusted, and bring them to a strange place with strange people and strange customs.

But most of all it was just a joy to see the return of the Olivia he'd once known. Last night she'd fluctuated from reserved to distant to tense, and this morning she'd been polite and professional. Hell, even when she'd been angry with him there'd been an aloofness that he'd never seen in her before.

But this was the Olivia of old. The one who got way too close to her patients. Who'd spend time at the end of a very long intern shift playing games or reading books to the kids in her charge, or stopping in at the shop to buy a favourite snack or a goofy toy for a child in her care.

Their bosses had frowned upon it, and he had teased her about it endlessly, but it was what made Olivia so good at what she did—she wasn't just their doctor, she was their friend.

That had, of course, led to tears on occasions. Every death or negative outcome she'd taken to heart. She'd considered herself a partner in a patient's journey and she'd felt it deeply when things went wrong.

Many a time he'd been a shoulder for her to cry on.

And he'd been worried last night, when she'd looked at him with such reserve and distance, that the old Olivia was gone forever. That maybe he'd been responsible for killing her off.

He was glad to see he hadn't.

She might have developed a harder shell, but it was good to know that she still had her gooey centre. It wasn't a particularly smart trait, or conducive to longevity in the profession, but as someone who also became a little too invested in the lives of the people he operated on Ethan recognised, on a subliminal level, that Olivia Fairchild was a kindred spirit.

It was why he'd chosen the army and humanitarian work over the more lucrative field of cosmetic surgery, unlike his father.

Because people mattered.

Ethan took a steadying breath and walked into the room. 'This looks like fun,' he said.

Olivia started at the sound of his voice and Ama, who took her cues in this strange new world from Olivia, shrank into her mother's arms, quickly pulling the headscarf covering the right side of her face closer, patting it, checking its position.

'Ethan,' Olivia said, scrambling off the bed. 'I thought you weren't going to be here until after lunch.' She turned quickly to Ama and smiled at the girl, who was still a bundle of nerves. 'It's okay,' she assured her, and Dali, the interpreter, repeated the assurances to Ama and her mother in their own language. 'This is the doctor I was telling you about. Dr Ethan.'

Ethan smiled as Ama peeked out at him from

her mother's shoulder. 'Very pleased to meet you, Ama,' he said, bowing slightly.

The girl's gaze darted to Olivia, and Olivia nodded and smiled again. She moved closer to Ethan, conscious of his tall breadth in her peripheral vision, trying to divorce herself from the sexual pull of him as she placed her hand on his forearm. 'We are old friends,' she said to Ama. 'We did our training together, here at this hospital.'

Ethan nodded. 'We sure did. Olivia used to tell us stories about having a pet kangaroo at home in Australia.'

That elicited a small smile from Ama and Olivia gave Ethan a grateful squeeze on the arm before she dropped her hand. Ethan's bedside manner had always been fantastic, but it had been a long time since she'd been familiar with his doctoring skills. A lot of surgeons tended not to be very good with their people skills.

Olivia introduced Ethan to Dali and to Ril, Ama's mother. He was at his charming best, but she was still nervous as to how he was going to go forward with Ama. Olivia knew he needed to see her face, but she also knew he needed to approach it very carefully.

'You like chequers?' Ethan said to Ama.

She gave a slight nod after Dali had translated.

'Do you mind if I watch while you and Olivia play?'

Ama looked at her mother, as the interpreter translated, and then at Olivia, who smiled. Very slightly she nodded her head.

'Excellent,' he said, smiling down at Ama.

Ethan drew up a chair opposite Dali on the same side of the bed. It was the side of Ama's defect and he was hoping that she'd become engrossed enough in the game to drop the fabric so he could get a good look. He was going to need a much closer examination before he operated, but for today he had to build some trust and he was happy to stay hands-off.

Two hours later Ethan knew a lot more than any photo could tell him about Ama's defect. Sure enough the girl had forgotten about trying to shield her face from him after about fifteen minutes, and he'd been able to get a much more thorough feel for the mechanics of what he was dealing with as the scarf slackened.

The extent of the destruction of her facial tissue and the functional impairment of her mouth and jaw were clinically challenging. He was going to need extensive imaging, but he was sure it was going to involve maxilla and palate losses as well.

It was shocking to look at. Ama essentially had a huge hole in the right side of her face, exposing the inside of her mouth, her jaw and nasal cavity. It was all the more shocking because it was a perfectly treatable condition caught early enough.

He knew from Olivia's briefing and studying Ama's chart that her NOMA had started the way it always did—with a simple mouth ulcer when she'd been four years old. But poor nutrition and poor oral hygiene had led to the ulcer developing quickly into full-blown NOMA. Her cheek had begun to swell and over the course of a few days it had developed blackish furrows as the gangrene set in. It had festered over weeks, forming horrible scabs. When the scabs had finally fallen away, she'd had a gaping hole in her face.

But Ama was one of the lucky ones—she'd survived. Ninety per cent of sufferers—usually children—didn't.

Just looking at Ama as she played chequers with Olivia swamped Ethan with a sense of hopelessness. NOMA *was* the face of poverty in poor, underdeveloped countries. And young children living in such extreme conditions where malnutrition was rife were at the highest risk.

He glanced at Olivia. The jacket she'd worn this morning to the debrief had long been discarded and her pencil skirt had rucked up her thighs slightly as she sat on the bed with her legs tucked up to one side. Her long-sleeved blouse fell softly against her breasts and was rolled up to the elbows. The top three buttons, which had been primly fastened all the way to the collar this morning, were now undone and gaping occasionally to reveal flashes of cleavage.

She looked perfectly at home and one hundred per cent unaffected by Ama's facial deformity as she played chequers. As if Ama was just another of her patients. But he knew Olivia's gooey centre well, and he knew she would be distressed by what this little girl had been through and the suffering she must face on a daily basis.

She glanced at him then and it was confirmed. Her gaze was a melted puddle of warm chocolate and it was begging him for help. To *do* something. To *fix* it.

And in that moment he'd have fixed it with his own bare hands if it had been within his power.

Instead he smiled at her and nodded.

He stood and smiled down at Ama and her mother. 'I'm going to get some tests organised,' he said, nodding reassuringly. 'They'll do them after lunch and Olivia will be with you the whole time, right?' he said, glancing at Olivia who had scrambled off the bed and was standing next to him.

'Right,' Olivia said, also smiling and nodding at Ama. 'I'm just going outside with Ethan for a moment,' she said. 'I won't be long.' She narrowed her eyes and wagged her finger playfully at Ama. 'Don't you cheat.'

Ama grinned.

Olivia was conscious of Ethan's big silent presence by her side as they walked out together. It was just like the old days—walking side by side through the Lighthouse.

Complete with the same old awareness. That delicious little frisson.

Which was pointless and useless and completely inappropriate!

'Thank you,' she said as they stepped into the corridor. 'You were very good with her.'

Ethan brushed off the compliment with a shrug. 'I think she'll be happy with the result.'

Ama was always going to have scarring and obvious skin grafting all her life, but he was confident they could close her oral and nasal cavities so she could swallow and eat properly and look more or less like other girls of her age.

Olivia smiled at him. 'I know she will.'

Ethan sucked in a breath at her full-wattage smile. It was the first one she'd given him in over a decade and he'd forgotten how deadly they were. 'I'll get the X-rays and MRI organised for this afternoon,' he said briskly, trying to dispel the strange tightness in his throat. 'We'll also need a full battery of blood tests.'

She put her hand on his arm as she'd done earlier. 'Again. Thank you. Will you ring me when you have the results?'

The fact that he hadn't yet apologised to her weighed on his conscience as she looked at him as if he'd discovered a cure for cancer. But as they stepped aside to let an orderly with a wheelchair pass Ethan knew that a hospital corridor wasn't the best place for it either.

'How about we go to Drake's for dinner and we can discuss it further there? I can bring my laptop and the images on a stick.'

Olivia blinked. 'Drake's is still around?' They'd been regulars at the bar during their time at the Lighthouse.

Ethan nodded. 'Drake's has been an institution around here for over a hundred years. There'd be a riot at the clinic if they shut down!'

Olivia laughed. Considering how many of Drake's clientele were hospital staff, Ethan was probably right. She hesitated, though. Being back with Ethan amongst so many familiar memories probably wasn't a good thing. Maybe she should try and limit that?

'Come on,' he persisted. 'You want to see the scans, and we've both gotta eat, right?'

Olivia couldn't fault his logic. 'That's true.'

'I'm seeing clients until six tonight, so how about I meet you there about six-thirty?'

She nodded before she changed her mind. 'Okay.'

Ethan waved to Olivia from the booth table he'd claimed when she arrived ten minutes late. He watched her wend her way through the early evening crowd. The cool night air had put some pink into her cheeks, reminding him of strawberries and cream.

He shook his head as the thought lodged in his brain. *Strawberries and cream?* For crying out loud—he'd be writing freaking poetry next!

'Sorry I'm late,' she said as she stopped in front of their booth and stripped her duffle coat and jacket off, revealing the blouse from earlier. His gaze drifted to her cleavage and those three little buttons, still undone.

'No worries,' he said as he forced his eyes upwards. 'I took the liberty of ordering you a glass of wine. You still like to drink Shiraz when it's cold outside?' he asked, indicating the glass of wine.

Olivia blinked at the glass, surprised he'd remembered. She probably shouldn't be—he'd always been a details man. But still, it had been ten years, and given the *true* nature of their previous relationship she was surprised he'd even bothered remembering in the first place.

'Oh, yes—thanks…' she said, settling into the booth opposite, pushing the bitterness aside. It was a long time ago and she was over him and the games he'd played.

Olivia took a sip and noticed the open laptop. 'That the scan?' she asked.

Ethan nodded. 'Yep.'

'Well, show us, then,' she said, placing her glass back on the table. 'I've been dying to know how fully the NOMA has invaded and the true extent of the damage.'

Ethan looked over the rim of his beer glass at Olivia. The scans were very interesting, and he could only imagine how someone as invested as Olivia would be desperate to pore over them, but first things first.

He shut the laptop lid and took a steadying breath. 'In a moment,' he said. 'There's something I have to say first.'

Olivia glanced at him. His voice was deadly serious and her heart pounded like a gong in her chest. *What the...?*

'I owe you an apology.'

She opened her mouth to say something but Ethan cut her off with a slice of his hand through the air.

'Please, Olivia, I need to get this out.'

He'd been rehearsing it all afternoon and he was grateful that she closed her mouth and let him get on with it.

'I'm very sorry for what happened ten years ago. For my reprehensible behaviour. For the way I used you and hurt you. For involving you in something that I shouldn't have. Basically, I'm sorry for being a total...jerk. There is absolutely no excuse for my behaviour. And I'm not expecting your forgiveness. I don't blame you if you hate me. I just want to be able to clear the air so we can work together. With the budding partnership between Fair Go and the clinic we're going to be seeing each other quite a bit, and I don't want it to be awkward between us. At least not because I haven't apologised, anyway.'

Ethan's heart was pounding when he'd finished and he grabbed his beer for a deep, long swallow as Olivia sat like a stunned mullet in her seat.

# CHAPTER FOUR

OLIVIA BLINKED AT the most comprehensive apology she'd ever received. Her fingers tightened around the stem of her wineglass as she was sucked back to the emotional tumult of that time.

He *had* acted reprehensibly. He *had* been a jerk. He'd hurt her. He'd broken her heart. Just… taken it and stomped all over it.

She'd never loved anyone as she'd loved Ethan Hunter.

He'd certainly made her wary of ever letting anyone in again. In fact she'd never really let anyone in since. Sure, she'd dated. She hadn't become some born again virgin. But she'd never given her heart to anyone else. And that was all because of Ethan. Mostly because he'd damaged it so badly, but also because, deep down, she'd measured every other guy against him.

And none of them had measured up.

Yes, the irony that a jerk had been her yardstick was not lost on her. But even though his motives for being with her had been grubby, his treatment of her had always been exemplary.

They'd had so much fun—being with him had been the best time of her life.

Ethan couldn't bear it as the silence stretched between them and she just kept staring at him. What was going on inside her head?

'Olivia?'

Olivia dragged herself back from the past, her gaze focusing on *this* Ethan. The thirty-five-year-old version. He was seeking forgiveness. Seemed to *need* it, if the intensity of his gaze was any kind of indication. Was it purely about Ama and their having to work together or was there a more personal absolution he was seeking?

'I don't hate you,' she said, picking up the glass of wine and taking a sip.

Even when her heart had been haemorrhaging she hadn't hated him.

'Hate implies strong emotion and the truth is I don't feel anything for you, Ethan. Not any more. It was ten years ago. We're different people, a lot has happened, and I've been over you for a long time. But you're right—we do need to work together, so clearing the air is good and I appreciate your *very* comprehensive apology. Thank you.'

Ethan knew he should feel relieved, and he did. But her admission that she felt nothing for him was startling.

*Nothing?*

Seeing her again had aroused a whole host of feelings. Nostalgia, apprehension, uncertainty. Hope. Worry.

Guilt.

And when she'd touched him last night—need, desire, lust.

It certainly hadn't been *nothing.* After a decade apart and their turbulent history how was *nothing* even possible?

But she was looking at him with such assuredness. The same old Liv, but different. The emotion and the connection he'd witnessed at the hospital earlier, that she'd been known for, were nowhere to be seen.

Well…if that was the way she wanted to play it. She was, after all, the wronged party.

'No,' he said, reaching out to cover her hand with his. 'Thank you.'

Olivia looked down at their joined hands. She'd used to dream that they'd be this amazing his-and-hers medical team—just like her parents. Living and loving and sharing. Growing old together. She'd been such a fool.

And she wouldn't go there again.

She pulled her hand away. 'Don't,' she said.

Ethan frowned at her abrupt withdrawal. 'I'm sorry… I didn't mean… That wasn't…'

'Accepting your apology does not mean that we're going to pick up where we left off, Ethan.'

Ethan quirked an eyebrow. *Whoa.* 'I didn't think it did.'

Olivia didn't care how egotistical she sounded. She needed to put it out there. Ethan was still as handsome as he'd always been. Probably even more so now life and experience had given his good looks a devastating depth.

Not to mention those fascinating shadows in his eyes.

'I know you,' she said. 'I know how it starts. So just don't…'

Ethan blinked. Did she think he was using his apology as a segue into some kind of pass? He knew he didn't exactly hold the moral high ground with her, but her insinuation was pretty damn insulting. 'Well, surely,' he said, withdrawing his hand and wrapping it around his beer, 'for someone who feels *nothing* that won't be an issue.'

Olivia was surprised at the bitterness of his tone. Had she annoyed him by her deliberate choice of words?

Too bad.

She'd been lying about the nothing, of course. Her body had been in a complete jumble for the past twenty-four hours. She *wished* she felt nothing. The way she had after the tears and the anger and the heavy sense of loss had all passed and she'd gone through life on autopilot. *Nothing* felt far preferable to the other stuff. It hurt less.

She'd gone there too, after her parents had been so cruelly snatched away. She'd craved the pain-free bubble of *nothing* back then. And had spent way too long inside it.

'Just putting my cards on the table. You and I aren't going to happen. Not going there. Not going there ever again. *Never, ever.*'

Ethan had an absurd urge to laugh at her emphatic denials. But he didn't think that would be appreciated. 'Are you trying to convince me or yourself?'

Olivia shivered as the low, gravelly note in his voice slid along the muscle fibres deep inside her belly. Their gazes locked for a brief moment and in those seconds she saw the golden flecks in his eyes flare to life as if a match had been struck.

And she felt a corresponding flare in those muscle fibres as they smouldered, then flickered to life.

'Just promise me it won't happen,' she said, desperate as heat spread through her belly. 'Say it out loud. I need to hear you say it.'

Ethan wanted to reach across the table and yank her sexy mouth right on to his. Okay, she didn't want anything to happen between them, and after he'd screwed up so badly last time he owed her that at least.

But, damn—it was all he *could* think about now.

*And he despised himself a little bit more.*

'I promise.' And he meant it. He raised his beer glass. 'Here's to *never, ever.*'

Olivia clinked her glass to his, feeling relieved and mollified. 'Good,' she said, taking a decent swallow of Shiraz. 'Now, show me the damn scan.'

They pored over the images for the next half-hour until their meals arrived. They talked about Ama's interesting facial anatomy, forever altered by the gangrenous infection. They talked about the staged repair and the different surgical approaches open to them. About anaesthetic options and the pros and cons of different types of grafting. About the potential complications.

During dinner they discussed timeframes and the team they'd need. They also touched on Ama's long-term recuperation and eventual follow-up. By the time their meals were finished they'd just about talked themselves through every aspect of Ama's care.

Olivia placed her cutlery on her empty plate and checked her watch—almost eight o'clock. If she left now she could be at the hospital before Ama went to sleep.

'You have somewhere to be?' Ethan asked as he drained the dregs of his second beer.

Olivia looked up. 'Sorry…yes… Do you mind? I've been reading some English books to Ama every night. She loves Dr Seuss, although I have no idea how much she understands.'

'I think Dr Seuss transcends language barriers,' Ethan said.

Olivia smiled. 'Yes, I think you might be right. It's just so good seeing her laugh, being a kid, you know?'

Ethan nodded. He'd been in a lot of places where children had to grow up too early. Where going to school and kicking a ball around weren't options. Where the innocence of childhood was usurped by the harsh realities of war and poverty.

His mind wandered to Aaliyah. To how she'd despaired about the children too.

So like Olivia in many ways.

'Yeah. I know.' He stood and grabbed his jacket, shrugging off the memory, refusing to compare. 'Come on, then, I'll walk with you.'

Olivia stood too. 'It's okay, it's not far. I'll be fine.'

'Liv,' Ethan said, 'I'm not going to let you walk the streets of London at night by yourself—especially when the Lighthouse is on my way home.'

Olivia's breath hitched as he reverted to the shortened version of her name. Did he remember when he'd started calling her that? Just after they'd first made love?

Had he even realised he'd done it?

'I've walked these streets many a time by myself, and way later than eight o'clock.' During her year in London she'd walked, bussed, tubed all over, at all hours of the day and night.

'Not when I was around, you didn't.'

And it was true. Ethan always had been the perfect gentleman. Well, except for that one time when he'd dragged her into an alley on their way to her place and had his wicked way with her because neither of them had been able to wait.

She huffed out a little breath, annoyed at her brain for dusting off that particular memory. 'Fine. Lead on.'

They were out on the street in under a minute. It was chilly after the warmth of the bar and Olivia buttoned up her duffle coat, pleased for its impenetrable warmth as they turned in the direction of the hospital. Unlike the thick wool of her tights, it *was* keeping out the cold. Her warm breath misted in the air and she set a brisk pace as icy fingers wrapped around her legs.

'So tell me about Fair Go,' Ethan said, leaning heavily on his stick to keep up with her.

Olivia stumbled a little at the unexpected question and felt his steadying hand briefly at her elbow before he removed it. 'I'm sure if you search for it online you'll find all you need to know.'

Ethan didn't care that she didn't want to talk. He needed to. Because all he could think about at the moment was a particularly steamy incident in an alley not far from here, and that wasn't conducive to a platonic walk.

'And why would I do that when I have the charity director at my disposal?'

Olivia shrugged. 'I started it a couple of years ago… I'd just finished my second stint with *Médecins Sans Frontières*—'

'Wait,' Ethan interrupted, placing a hand on her arm and urging her to stop. 'You worked for Doctors Without Borders?'

Olivia drew to a halt. 'Yes,' she said.

She remembered how Ethan had often talked about wanting to take his surgical skills into conflict zones. She had already been marinated in her parents' humanitarian works, and Ethan's fervour had easily infected Olivia. He'd hated—been embarrassed by—his father's lucrative cosmetic surgery clinic when there was so much suffering in the world, and had been determined to make a difference.

She'd hoped they'd do it together. Like her parents had. And then things had ended and she'd thrown herself instead into her parents' work in remote areas of Australia. But when they'd been lost she'd needed something more. She'd needed to get away.

To be totally absorbed in something other than her own grief.

'What can I say…?' she said, pulling away. 'You inspired me.'

Ethan let her walk on for a bit, the belt on her royal blue coat pulled tight against the cold, emphasising her petite frame. He'd had no idea she'd followed through with their fledgling plans to join the famed international organisation. He'd assumed they'd fallen through when their relationship had ended.

He should have known—she'd always been strong-willed, her petite physicality belying the strength of her character.

'Where did you go?' he asked as he caught her up.

'Africa,' she said, keeping her gaze dead ahead. It was bad enough that he filled up her peripheral vision with all his sexy, haggard broadness.

'And that's where you got the idea for Fair Go?'

Olivia nodded. 'I saw a lot of kids with terrible conditions falling through the cracks because they weren't classed as *emergency* or *life-threatening*. But they did affect the quality of those kids' lives. And why should they have to suffer because they had the misfortune to be born into poverty? Why shouldn't they have the same expectations as kids in the western world?'

Ethan heard the husky note creep into Olivia's voice as they stopped at a red signal and waited to cross the road. 'I agree,' he murmured.

The Hunter Clinic was working with charities all over the world, trying to redress that balance.

'There are a lot of charity and aid organisations out there that have a particular focus on certain regions or diseases or conditions or gender. And I get that—I do. There's just not enough charity dollars to go around.'

She turned to face him slightly.

'But it doesn't make it *fair*,' she said. 'I want to be able to give the children who fall through the cracks a chance at a better life too. They deserve a fair go too.'

Ethan nodded. Of course they did. So Olivia Fairchild was going to see to it. Good on her.

'I'm assuming your parents are the main benefactors?' he asked. 'They must be very proud of you.'

Like himself, Olivia came from a wealthy background. It had been one of the many things they'd had in common. Except Olivia's parents had turned their backs on lucrative practices and devoted their time to isolated communities as flying doctors.

Olivia was grateful that the light changed just then and they were able to cross the street as quick, hot tears welled in her eyes. She blinked them back. It wasn't Ethan's fault that he didn't know about her parents' tragic demise. She hadn't told him, and it was hardly as if their deaths had made international headlines.

She swallowed the lump in her throat. 'Yes. I got the money from my parents,' she said. 'And I have some good people I trust looking after the financial side of things.'

Ethan nodded. He knew how important it was to have trustworthy people involved in things like this. 'Well, Ama is very lucky to have someone looking out for her and willing to give *her* a fair go.'

Olivia suppressed a snort. He had no idea. Ama might be happy and bright now, but that was not how she'd been the day she'd first met the girl and her mother on a dirt street.

Ethan glanced at Olivia. Her brow was furrowed. 'You're frowning,' he said, shoving his hands in his pockets. 'Are you worried about Ama? Don't be. Everything's going to work out fine. Trust me.' He grinned as her frown continued. 'I'm a surgeon. And I'm *good*.'

Olivia looked up at him, his chiselled features filling her vision. His smile sucked the breath from her lungs. *Oh, he was good, all right.* They were probably a metre apart but he felt much closer—Ethan and his indomitable confidence had always managed to fill up the space between them.

She *was* worried about Ama. But not about the procedure or his ability to perform it. She had one hundred per cent faith in Ethan's capabilities and she knew Ama would be a very different girl by the time her multiple surgeries were done.

'I know,' she said. 'It's just…afterwards I'm worried about. When she heads back home again.

You and I both know she's still not going to look like she did before NOMA, and that makes her... vulnerable.'

Ethan slowed a little. 'You're worried she'll still be ostracised?'

Olivia slowed too. 'Yes. And I'm worried that her uncle will still force her into marriage.'

Ethan blinked. 'What? She's *nine*, Olivia,' he snorted.

'That wasn't stopping him the day I found her.'

Ethan felt a cold fist close around his heart as Olivia's words sunk in. 'I beg your pardon?'

Olivia shuddered, thinking back to the horrible altercation she'd witnessed. She vividly recalled the taste of vomit in her mouth when the interpreter had finally sorted out what was happening.

'The day I found Ama her uncle, who was the head of her household since Ama's father had died the year before, was giving her away to a man who looked at least forty. She was crying and clinging to her mother, and her mother was crying and begging her brother to reconsider.'

Another rush of emotion filled Olivia's chest.

She shook her head against it, tried to push it back, but the memory was still so acute. How could anyone force a *nine*-year-old girl to *marry*? The thought was utterly vile.

Olivia wasn't naive—she knew awful stuff like that happened in places that the world didn't care to know about—but confronting it first-hand had been wrenching. Caught up in the rekindled horror of it, she turned to Ethan.

'You should have seen them,' she said. 'They were…clutching each other in the middle of this…street. It wasn't even a street, really—just this dirt…pathway. They were both so skinny and desperate and…wailing. Ril was wailing and holding on tight as this…disgusting old man with gnarled hands and three yellow teeth pulled at Ama's arm.'

Olivia halted, oblivious to the people walking behind her, caught up for a moment in the heat and utter despair that symbolised so much of Africa for her. It had been horrible. The consequences for Ama had she not intervened were still too much for her to bear.

Ethan gently took her elbow, moving her out

of the path of other pedestrians who were bustling around them.

'It was terrible, Ethan,' she said, only vaguely aware that they were standing on the first step of the very grand entrance to one of the many clinics that populated the area. The Lighthouse was only two blocks away now.

'It's okay,' he murmured. The distress on Olivia's face squeezed his gut tight and he wanted to make it better.

Olivia shook her head. 'No, it's not,' she said.

'No,' he agreed. 'I'm sorry. It's not.'

She looked up at him. Muted light shone through the glass side panels of the grand doorway and fell over the planes and angles of his face. 'I couldn't leave her,' she said. 'I couldn't...'

Ethan nodded. 'Of course not.' His hand was still at her elbow and he gave it a gentle squeeze. 'What did you do?'

She shrugged helplessly. 'I gave him all the money I had on me and told him to get lost. And then I didn't let her out of my sight.'

Ethan smiled down at her. The light from inside lit her face and her eyes glittered with indignation. She looked fierce. Like a mother bear. He could just imagine her, furious and fearless, defending a child, standing up to a man in a hugely patriarchal society. Telling him to get lost.

'That was brave,' he murmured.

The compliment slid into all the places Olivia had forgotten about. Places that Ethan had always kept alive and humming. They were standing close on the step, closer than when they'd been walking, and she could smell the beer on his breath and the spice of his cologne.

'Dali called it stupid.'

Ethan chuckled. 'Well, it was probably a little of that as well.'

His low, sexy laugh was just the right timbre to produce an army of goose bumps and a funny little pull somewhere in the vicinity of her belly button. 'I was scared witless,' she admitted. 'But…what else could I do?'

Even now the thought of Ama's fate had Olivia just walked away was too distressing to think about.

Ethan shook his head. Her gaze was so raw and

her question so earnest. 'You're a good woman, Olivia Fairchild. You always were.'

And he meant it. It buzzed through his veins, echoed around his head and filled up his chest. He was proud just to know her, to have a chance to know her again, and before he could stop himself he'd stepped in close, slid his hands onto her waist and dropped his mouth to hers.

And it felt good as she opened to him. Easy and sexy and right. Just as it always had. Her lips soft, her taste and her scent stirring old memories, urging him to go deeper, to pull her closer.

And he did.

Olivia temporarily lost her way as the taste and the touch and the smell of him wiped out all her common sense. It was as if she'd been transported back to their first kiss a decade ago. A kiss that had started out as a crazy, tired comfort thing, after a long, harrowing night shift together, and quickly became something quite different.

Something that had made absolute sense.

She slid her palms up the front of his jacket, smoothing and sculpting the muscles she knew lay beneath, clutching at his lapels as she tried to recapture that long-ago crazy/sane moment to take her away from the dirt and heat and poverty of Africa.

The tragedy of Ama and girls just like her.

The tragedy of her parents.

The tragedy of them.

Ethan groaned as Olivia deepened the kiss, opening her mouth wider, her tongue hot, dancing a wild tango with his.

'Liv…' His hands slid down to cup her bottom as his groin caught fire.

Olivia protested against his mouth as common sense wrenched her away from him.

*One word.*

Just one word and he'd yanked her back to reality.

'Damn it!' She pushed on his chest, stepping back, stepping out of his arms, sucking in air, breathing hard.

*What was she doing? What the hell was she doing?* Kissing Ethan again. Ethan, who was even more messed-up than he'd been a decade ago. Ethan with the shadows in his eyes.

Ethan whom she had to work with.

'You promised,' she hissed at him.

Ethan's head reeled from the abrupt disconnect. His head buzzed with the sexual high even as shame and guilt flooded over the top, smothering it very effectively.

He hadn't betrayed Aaliyah's memory in a year.

And here he was, kissing an ex-girlfriend on a public street like some grubby teenage boy.

Olivia glared at him, mad at herself but madder still at him. She'd be a bloody fool to get involved with Ethan Hunter again.

She pushed him hard in the chest. 'You promised *never, ever,*' she accused. 'We toasted it!'

'I'm…sorry,' he said, trying to pull himself together for Olivia as he battled his own demons. 'I…got carried away.'

*Olivia knew the feeling.*

But she was too angry to see his side right now. Too angry with herself. One touch of his lips and her resolve just disappeared.

She had to get away. She had to see Ama, for God's sake. It was the whole reason they were out on the street together in the first place. Not for some public necking session.

'I have to get to the hospital,' she said tersely.

Ethan nodded. 'Of course. I'll see you in the morning,' he said, knowing the Lighthouse was close enough now for her to get there without his company.

But it didn't stop him watching her as she hurried away without a backward glance.

# CHAPTER FIVE

BY THE TIME he entered his apartment ten minutes later Ethan had called himself every name under the sun. He'd kissed Olivia after expressly promising not to start anything. And even though she'd kissed him back it was unforgivable.

It seemed he was destined to behave unforgivably around Olivia.

And what about his vows to Aaliyah? Forgotten in one mad moment. What kind of a man did that make him?

Guilt chewed at his gut as he splashed whisky into a glass. Guilt over kissing Olivia. For *wanting* to kiss Olivia. For forgetting about the woman he'd loved—the woman he'd left behind in a Godforsaken part of the world, whom he'd promised he'd be back for.

*Another broken promise.*

Ethan's brain seethed and boiled like molten

lava in a volcanic cauldron as he stared morosely into the depths of the amber liquid in the crystal tumbler. How could he have betrayed the memory of Aaliyah? Yes, she was gone. She was dead and he was alive. But it had only been a year.

One lousy year.

How could he have forgotten his promise to her the day he'd asked her to marry him? That he would love her only, be faithful to her always?

And what about the silent pledge he'd taken the day he'd woken up in the hospital to the news of Aaliyah's death? That he was done with love. Done with relationships.

Done with emotion. With feeling. With passion.

Those things had died with Aaliyah and he'd literally felt the bands of cold steel wrapping around his heart as he'd sworn never to get involved again, never to love again. Hell, he'd welcomed them. They and the scars on his legs were his reminder that the women he loved tended to leave him.

His mother. Aaliyah.

He'd resigned himself to a solo life. Was he

happy? No. But how could he be after what had happened to him? And where had happiness got him anyway? He was…content. He and Leo were in a good place, he was going to be an uncle soon, and he was doing good work. Important work that meant something to him.

And now Olivia had walked back into his life.

Ethan swirled the whisky in the glass. *Damn her.* Damn her for getting too close. Again. For making him remember what it felt like to be a man.

To want a woman. To want to feel her, taste her.

He hadn't needed that in his life. And he sure as hell hadn't missed it. The desire for physical affection had been non-existent.

Couldn't she just have stayed away? Left him with his ghosts and demons? He'd grown used to them for company and he'd been just fine here in his shell.

And yet with one look and that gut-wrenching shimmer of emotion in her expressive gaze he'd wanted more. Just like that she'd wormed her way under his skin—just like ten years ago, when he'd only been supposed to be using her to throw in Leo's face but she'd come to mean more.

Even now he couldn't get her out of his head. Couldn't stop replaying their kiss over and over. He could still taste her, feel the curve of her waist embedded into his palm. Feel the tension in his belly and the tightness in his groin.

He shut his eyes, desperately trying to recall Aaliyah. Her bronzed skin, her midnight eyes, her calming touch. But all he saw was Olivia.

A surge of anger and frustration welled in his chest as Ethan fought another battle. The glass felt good in his hand—heavy. Reeking of money and class. As did the whisky. And he wanted nothing more than to knock it back. Have a second. A third. But Olivia was still in his head. As was her taunt from last night. Packing a bigger punch than it had already.

*'I'm sure that's exactly how your father started out.'*

Damn it!

He shook his head, letting the rage bubble up and out. Swinging wildly around, he threw the heavy crystal glass at the opposite wall. The crash was loud, as was the inevitable harsh shatter as shards of glass and liquid slid down the wall.

Ethan stood for long moments just staring at the mess, his heart pounding in his chest. He didn't feel any better. He still wanted a drink. He still wanted Olivia.

*Damn it!*

He stalked to the nearby gym set-up that Lizzie had organised for him back when she'd been his home visit nurse. She'd been determined not to just dress his wounds and check he was taking his medication but to bully him into doing his physio so he could strengthen his legs and stop brooding inside the house.

Ethan sat at the leg press machine. And took out his frustrations on it.

Olivia knew it was her turn to apologise this morning. After tossing and turning through another sleepless night she knew she was as much to blame for the kiss as Ethan.

No, she hadn't made the first move. But she hadn't immediately pushed him away either. She hadn't told him no or slapped his face. In fact she'd opened her mouth wider, invited him in, stepped in nearer, put her hands on him. For God's sake, she'd grabbed hold of his lapels and dragged him closer!

She might not have asked for it but she'd definitely encouraged its continuation. So *she* would be the one saying sorry, as soon as he walked through Ama's door this morning.

Thankfully he didn't make her wait too long, showing up at the room at eight-thirty in a set of blue Theatre scrubs.

And for a moment Olivia lost her breath.

She'd forgotten how damn good the man looked in blue. It was such a girly, sky-blue too, and yet somehow he oozed masculinity. Maybe it was the way he filled them out. The breadth of his shoulders, the narrowness of his hips… Or maybe it was the rough-looking salt and pepper whiskers at his jaw.

He shot her a hesitant smile and a quick nod before he turned his attention to Ama and her mother. She was watching something loud and animated on the overhead television, scarf firmly in place. There was no way she could possibly follow the plot—it didn't even make a whole lot of sense in English—but she seemed utterly engrossed nonetheless, even bursting out laughing occasionally.

Olivia watched as he pulled up a chair by Ama's bed and sat down facing the television, also taking in the cartoon.

'What's that dog doing?' he asked Ama, and Dali dutifully interpreted.

They chatted back and forth through Dali about the television show, as if he had all the time in the world instead of a Theatre list that probably started in thirty minutes. When an ad break came he took advantage, and Olivia listened as he explained to Ril and Ama, in clear simple terms, what the tests had shown and how they were going to proceed. It was pretty much an abbreviated layman's version of what she and Ethan had talked about last night in the bar.

*Before they'd ruined the evening by letting their past rear its ugly head.*

'I'm putting a team together now and we're going to do the first surgery on Wednesday next week,' he said, and waited for Dali to translate. 'The second one probably three or four weeks later.'

Ril, who was sitting on the bed next to her daughter, nodded and asked a question.

'Ril would like to know if Olivia will be one of the surgeons,' Dali said.

'Absolutely,' Olivia piped up. 'Let him just try and stop me!'

There was a lightness to her tone, but Ethan heard the undercurrent loud and clear. Did she think he'd try and block her after what had happened between them last night? He knew how much Olivia wanted to be involved—he would never do that.

He turned to reassure her. 'Of course Olivia will be there,' he said, smiling at her before turning back to Ama. 'I seem to remember she was an excellent surgeon and I have every faith she's only got better.'

Olivia, who'd been nervous of Ethan's answer, relaxed. 'I have,' she said with a smile for Ama's benefit.

She'd assured Ama she would be there with

her the whole time, and even if Ama was asleep and not aware of her being there Olivia intended to honour her promise.

The questions went back and forth for a while longer and Olivia was impressed that Ethan was prepared to sit and answer every one—not hurrying, just being thorough, which was an exercise in patience when the whole process took twice as long with an interpreter.

When the questions seemed exhausted Ethan looked at the little girl and hoped he'd won her trust enough for his next request. He was conscious of what Olivia had told him last night—conscious that Ama's trust of men, particularly those in authority, must be very shaky.

But he really did need to examine the operative area a little more closely. He'd been careful not to leap into that too early, but he wanted to do some computer modelling over the weekend so it was important to be able to assess the current state of the oral cavity, the health of the mucosa and gums—something an MRI couldn't tell him.

He turned back to face Olivia. He needed her help now. 'I was hoping that Ama might let me have a look inside her mouth now?' he said. He looked at Ama. 'What do you say?'

Olivia took her cue as Dali spoke to Ama. She moved to the opposite side of the bed from Ethan, perched herself on the mattress and took Ama's hand with an encouraging smile for both her and her mother.

'Ethan's going to use a special light, like I was telling you,' Olivia said, 'to have a look inside your mouth so he gets the operation right.'

Ama started to look apprehensive and Olivia gave her hand a squeeze. 'It's okay. It won't hurt, and Mum and I and Dali will all be right here with you.'

Ama looked from Ethan to Olivia then back again, in that solemn way of hers with her big brown eyes. That look always broke Olivia's heart. Ama had eyes that had already seen too much heartache and suffering for one so young.

'See?' Ethan said, pulling a small pen torch out of his pocket and flicking it on, placing it in Ama's hand for her to get a feel for its harmlessness.

Ama looked down at the instrument. She

turned it over in her hands and then turned it so the light shone directly in her eyes. She squinted and pulled the light away. She turned to look at her mother, then back at the torch, shining it in her face again. This time she squinted and gave a nervous giggle.

'This is what you'll look like,' Ethan said, taking the torch out of her hand, opening his mouth, placing the lit end against his cheek and then closing it again. His cheek glowed an eerie red and he waggled his eyebrows at her.

This time Ama laughed. As did Ril and Dali. Olivia's throat tightened at his ease with Ama, and for a moment she was transported back to the old days, when the torch-in-the-mouth thing had been one of their favourite games to play with the kids at the Lighthouse.

His bedside manner had always been second to none.

'See?' he said pulling it out, then wiping it over with an antiseptic wipe. 'It doesn't hurt at all.'

Ama pointed to Olivia and said something in her own language. Neither of them needed an interpreter to understand her meaning.

Olivia huffed out an exaggerated sigh, rolling her eyes as she held out her hand for the torch. 'If you insist,' she griped good-naturedly.

Ethan winked at her as he placed it in her open palm. His fingers brushed lightly against her and a little spark of heat ran up her arm. She glanced at him and wondered if he felt it too, but he was smiling at Ama.

Olivia flicked the torch on and popped it in her mouth. The acrid taste of antiseptic was bitter on her tongue but she ignored it, pushing the light into the mucosa of her cheek and closing her mouth around her. Her cheek dutifully glowed red and Ama laughed louder this time.

'Dali. Dali,' Ama said in her guttural accent, and Ethan laughed knowing there was going to be no quick way of doing this as both Dali and then Ril were also subjected to the trick, the torch being cleaned in between.

Consequently, when it came to the examination Ama submitted happily. Ethan was pleased to note that the oral mucosa looked relatively healthy and he took a few seconds to assess and familiarise himself with some of the landmarks he'd noted in the MRI.

But then the fun part came, when Olivia found a mirror and they spent ages flashing the light on and off inside Ama's unaffected cheek. Every time her cheek glowed red she laughed as if it was the funniest thing she'd ever seen. It was sobering to think that, sadly, in Ama's case it probably was.

'Okay, okay.' Ethan smiled. 'I've got to go but I'll be in to see you…' he waggled his fingers at Ama and the girl giggled '…every day.'

Ama reluctantly surrendered the torch, holding it out to him, but Ethan shook his head. 'It's a gift for you. Enjoy.'

Ama's eyes widened as Dali relayed the message and Olivia felt a wave of goose bumps march over her skin as Ama hugged it to her chest.

Olivia followed Ethan out through the door as he departed. She wanted to get the apology off her chest straight away. A bit like he had last night.

'Thanks so much for that,' she said as they

both watched Ama from the doorway, smiling as she flicked the light on and off and shone it on everything. 'Anyone would think you just gave her the sun.'

Ethan shrugged. Olivia was wearing a pair of snug jeans again today, and a fine woollen sweater that fell nicely against all the flesh beneath. It wasn't helping his resolve to keep his hands off. He'd thought about his rekindling sexual attraction to her a lot last night, and probably limiting their alone time together was wise.

'Plenty more where that came from,' he said.

Olivia nodded. She knew that drug reps alone kept doctors endlessly supplied with such knick-knacks. 'Well, you made her day.'

Hell, given where Ama came from, he'd probably made her entire life! She doubted the girl had ever received too many gifts of such a magical calibre.

Ethan cleared his throat as they both watched Ama continue to play with her new toy. 'About last night—'

'Oh, no,' Olivia said, quickly cutting him off as she turned to face him. 'Let me.'

Ethan eyed her warily. 'Let you what?'

'Apologise,' she said.

Ethan folded his arms. 'Liv...*I* was the one who kissed *you*, remember? After I'd just promised I wouldn't go there.'

Olivia shook her head, trying to shrug off the way he said her name and how it heated all the old familiar places. Unfortunately the way the fabric of his scrubs pulled around his shoulders and biceps didn't help with the heat problem.

With her heart already fluttering, and her cheeks already flushed at the delicate subject matter, heat was the last thing she needed.

The memory of the kiss sat between them like a big guilty secret, and she'd rather crawl over an acre of glass than have to discuss the way they'd erred last night—like a couple of kids sent to the naughty corner by their parents to talk over their behaviour. She was a grown woman and it was an embarrassing discussion to be having.

But she couldn't let him take the fall for it either.

She needed to own her part in it.

'Yes, I know,' she said. 'But I didn't exactly

stop you. I was as much to blame. Probably even more so if you consider my *never, ever* carry-on at the bar. I should have pulled back straight away. I should have…slapped your face,' she said, trying to make a joke to ease the awkwardness of the situation.

Much to her relief, Ethan eked out a half-smile. 'It's fine,' he dismissed. 'How about we both take equal responsibility and agree that being alone together is probably something we should avoid?'

Olivia let out a breath she hadn't been aware she was holding. She returned his half-smile with one of her own. 'That sounds like a good plan.'

Ethan nodded. 'Okay, then.'

'So… I take it I'm still okay to scrub in on some of your surgeries, though? I'm really keen to do what I can while I'm here, and now Ama and her mother are settled they're probably sick of the sight of me.'

Ethan grunted. He doubted that. Ama and Ril's faces lit up like a city skyline whenever Olivia entered the room. Given what she'd done for them, he didn't blame them.

He remembered a time when she'd made him

light up too. When he'd felt more for her than he'd ever anticipated.

But he had to admit to being curious about how Olivia had developed as a surgeon. And they could always do with more help.

The clinic's humanitarian programme ran on a tight budget—it had to when billing charities was involved. Having a third surgeon in an op was sometimes necessary—as it would be with Ama and other big cases—but usually not.

It was certainly not a luxury they could afford.

And Ethan didn't believe in wasting money—too much of that went on in charity circles as it was. The Hunter Clinic was opulent and wealthy, and the programme was lucky to have the free use of it and all its associated services—including the pro bono time of any of its surgeons.

But the charities involved paid for all the extra stuff that the Hunter Clinic couldn't provide—including any outside surgeons—and Ethan didn't believe in running up their bills like that unless it was completely necessary.

But Olivia was free. And a free surgeon was a gift he wasn't about to knock back.

'I have a big burn contracture release tomorrow. I could use an extra pair of hands with it.'

A little trill of excitement ran through Olivia at the thought of being back at the table again. It had been a few months since she'd picked up a scalpel and she'd missed it.

'Sounds great.'

Ethan nodded. 'I'll be able to introduce you to some of the team that will be working on Ama's op next week as well. Kara Stephens is helping me out tomorrow. She's a junior surgeon— another Aussie who's a real go-getter and has wanted in on Ama's surgery ever since she heard the first whisper about it. And Jock McNamara is the anaesthetist on my list in the morning and I want him for Ama's surgery. He does a lot of anaesthetics for the facio-maxillary ops and really knows his stuff.'

'It'll be great to meet some of the team,' Olivia enthused.

'Good,' Ethan said. 'List starts at eight-thirty at Princess Catherine's.'

'I'll be there.'

There was an awkward moment when they

both paused, waiting for the other to say something and then both realising simultaneously that the silence was growing.

'Right, then…' Ethan said. 'See you tomorrow, Liv.'

Olivia felt the emotional whammy again of what had been a very intimate connection between them. Liv had been the name he'd called her behind closed doors. The name he'd chanted in her ear as he moved deep inside her. The named he'd cried out as he came.

She couldn't be Olivia Fairchild if he reverted to Liv all the time. Olivia was a capable paediatric reconstructive surgeon. Olivia was a compassionate doctor who had put her skills and her heart on the line in Africa. Olivia was the director of Fair Go.

Liv was Ethan's friend. His confidante. His lover.

Liv was the woman who knew the depths of his pain and anger.

Liv was the woman who had loved him.

'Ethan.'

Her quiet call stopped him in his tracks and

Ethan turned to face her. She hadn't moved from the spot in the hallway where he'd left her. 'Yeah?'

'Please don't call me Liv...' she murmured.

He was tall and dark and handsome and she wanted to run straight into his arms. Being here, in this hospital with him, stirred too many memories. Unfortunately none of the bad ones. None of the things that had broken her.

'It's too...hard...it's too...familiar.'

Ethan nodded slowly. A heat unfurled inside his gut and travelled south. He hadn't even realised he'd said it. The name—the endearment—had come from somewhere way back in the past. From memories rich with laughter. And spoiled by the callousness of his youth.

If he was going to cling to Aaliyah, to the welcome familiarity of his grief and guilt, then Liv *could not* exist.

'I'm sorry,' he said, rubbing the back of his neck. 'I didn't realise...'

Olivia nodded. 'I know.'

Ethan regarded her for a moment or two. 'I

don't want this any more than you do, Olivia. I can't.'

She could tell from the dullness of his eyes that he was telling the truth. That his body was betraying him as much as hers was betraying her.

*Remember that, stupid foolish heart—he doesn't want this. Neither do you.*

'I know,' she said again.

They didn't say anything for a moment, and then Ethan said, 'See you in the morning,' and turned away.

Olivia watched him go, acutely aware of the contrast between a happy Ama to one side of her and the stoic set of Ethan's receding back to the other.

His choice of words intrigued her. *I can't.* 'Can't' implied more than a conflict of choice. 'Can't' implied something out of his control. Had he meant that? Or had it just been a slip of the tongue?

And if he had meant it, what exactly *did* it mean? Did it mean that he actually wasn't able to? Wasn't capable? Emotionally? Or had something happened to him physically on one of his tours? Maybe his injuries were more extensive than just his legs?

Could 'can't' mean that he wasn't able to perform sexually any more?

And why on earth would he think any woman worth her salt would give a damn about it?

Olivia gave herself a mental shake. What did it matter? She wasn't here to get involved in his life. To commiserate about any long-term effects of his war wounds or to kiss him better.

She was here for Fair Go. She was here for Ama.

And Ama was just one of the many kids she planned to bring to the UK for surgery. Several had already benefited, thanks to Fair Go and the generosity of the Hunter Clinic.

And that was what she needed to concentrate on.

Running a charity was a big freaking deal, involving serious money and financial responsibility, and she couldn't afford to drop the ball because some guy from a million years ago— who had, *by the way*, ground her heart into the dirt—looked at her with shadows in his eyes and called her Liv.

Ethan Hunter was a big boy who'd had his chance with her and blown it.

She wasn't his *Liv* any longer.

## CHAPTER SIX

ETHAN WAS SCRUBBING up at the sinks in the scrub room the next morning when Olivia bustled through the door.

'God, I'm so sorry,' she said, barely acknowledging him as she pulled up beside him and reached over to remove a mask out of the nearby box, tying it on in record time. 'I underestimated the time it would take me to get here, and the streets…'

She shook her head as she wrenched off her opal ring and shoved it into the pocket of her scrub trousers.

'I don't remember them being this busy ten years ago.'

She opened a sterile packaged scrub brush and flicked on the taps, wetting her arms from the fingertips to the elbows. She turned to look at him as her right hand attacked the nails on her left hand with the brush. She knew the scrub routine back to front and could do it blindfolded.

'When did it get so busy?'

Ethan blinked. Olivia had always been a chatter. Her ability to fill up a silence or engage a total stranger with her intelligent observations on any subject was one of the things that had drawn them together in the first place. She'd always blamed it on her single child status, remarking that chatter had been her defence against loneliness.

Certainly their stilted, awkward conversations over the past few days had been well out of character.

But she was in fine form this morning.

'It's London,' he said, smiling beneath his mask. 'The streets have always been busy.'

Olivia conceded his point as she turned back to inspect her work. A large window in front of them gave them direct visual access to the Theatre and Olivia noted that the patient was already on the table and was being draped.

She switched the scrubbing brush to the other hand. 'Well, it's a far cry from Africa, that's for sure.'

'True. Not a lot of giraffes in London,' he remarked dryly.

To his surprise she laughed. A laugh that came straight from her soul and ruffled the edges of a hundred different memories. Having her beside him like this again, in scrubs and a mask, her expressive eyes dominating—it was as if they'd never been apart.

It felt comfortable. Like old times.

As it could have always been if he hadn't been so angry and vengeful, so damn determined to lash out.

So he did the only thing he could do to distract himself from futile games of *what if.* He started talking about the case.

'Our patient today, Daleel, is a twenty-eight-year-old Somali man who suffered burns five years ago to over forty per cent of his body. Frankly, how he survived I'll never know, because he only had the most rudimentary of medical care.'

Olivia nodded. It was something she'd seen over and over during her time on the front line and working with various aid organisations in conjunction with Fair Go. Men, women and children who survived against all the odds—like Ama—but who were left permanently and hideously disfigured with absolutely no hope of leading a normal life.

'His right arm is fused to his torso, his right hand is badly contractured, and the severe scarring of his face and neck have led to a contracture that's pulling his whole head into a downward flexion.'

Ethan, at the end of his scrub, held his bent soapy arms out in front of him, hands up, elbows down, and dunked them under the spray tap. He watched as the water sluiced from his fingertips down his arms and dripped suds off his elbows into the sink.

'Think you can handle it?' he asked. The soap was all gone now, and he flicked the tap off with an elbow, then held his arms over the sink a little longer, waiting for his elbows to stop dripping.

'I think so,' Olivia said.

He glanced at her and for a moment their gazes met over the top of their masks and the sense of familiarity returned. Ethan straightened. 'See you in there,' he murmured.

Olivia was conscious of him in her peripheral vision, his sterile arms out in front of him, using his back to push open the swing doors. Then through the glass window she saw him emerge into the Theatre, hands still up and out from his body, striding towards the scrub nurse who was already masked, gowned and gloved and holding out a sterile towel for him to dry his hands.

She continued her scrub, watching Ethan go through the familiar routine of gowning and gloving. She'd never known a man to look so damn good in what was essentially a no-frills dress. The plainness of it just seemed to emphasise the broadness of his chest and the length of his frame. Some women got off on men who wore Armani suits. But she much preferred a man in Theatre garb.

And *damn* if Ethan didn't rock a pair of scrubs.

He chose that moment to glance up from checking the tray of instruments that had been placed near the patient, and their gazes locked as he looked directly at her. Olivia blushed, grateful for the camouflage of the mask. Had he been able to read her less than professional thoughts?

Was he remembering her fetish for a man in scrubs?

Did he remember that time she'd admitted to the erotic dream she'd had about him, involving an examination table, some handcuffs, a pair of scrubs and the very inventive use of a scalpel for removing said scrubs from his otherwise naked body?

They never did get round to enacting that particular fantasy...

The other surgeon—what had Ethan said her name was?—leaned in obliviously, asking him a question, and Olivia quickly dropped her gaze.

*What the hell was she doing?*

She was here to help give a man his life back. Not to have completely inappropriate, unprofessional and *graphic* thoughts about a highly respected surgeon.

Olivia dunked her arms under the water, watching the soapy residue disappear down the drain, and hoped to God her erotic thoughts would follow.

\* \* \*

Ethan entered Drake's the following Tuesday night with a spring in his step—not exactly easy to do with his limp. Tomorrow was Ama's operation and everyone at the clinic was psyched about it. The team was in place and raring to go, Kara could talk about nothing else, and he knew Olivia—although she was more subdued than the excitable junior surgeon—was also eager to get underway.

He knew how close she was to Ama's case.

Maybe she shouldn't be. Maybe it wasn't the professional thing to do. If something went wrong… But some cases just got to you—he knew that.

And nothing was going to go wrong.

The surgery tomorrow was complex, but they all knew what they were doing. And Ama's new life was just around the corner.

'Ethan!'

Ethan looked up to find Leo waving at him across the reasonably full bar. He was at a table with Olivia, Kara, and her fiancé, Declan Underwood—a plastic surgeon who also worked at the Hunter Clinic.

He made his way over to the group. He was supposed to be meeting Leo here for an after-work drink and a general catch-up. There'd been a fairly full surgical list the past five days and Ethan had only been into 200 Harley Street for a few hours on the weekend, to do the computer modelling for Ama's surgery.

But Leo liked to have a meeting once a week to discuss general Hunter Clinic business and Ethan had bunked out on the past two. He appreciated his brother wanting him involved now he was an active partner in the business, but Ethan had no doubt that Leo could and did run the clinic perfectly well without his input.

Hell, the man had dragged the sinking clinic out of the scandalous mire it had sunk into after their father's headline-grabbing drunken scene and subsequent death. He'd worked day and night not only to put it back into the red but into the hearts, minds and chequebooks of every A-lister in Europe and beyond.

The only decisions Ethan wanted to be consulted over were those that involved the humanitarian programme. Then he was all ears.

'I hope you don't mind us crashing your party.' Declan grinned, half standing and holding out his hand as Ethan pulled up at the table.

The man's Irish brogue seemed more pronounced tonight, and Ethan assumed it was due to the almost empty pint of Guinness sitting in front of him.

Ethan shook Declan's hand, nodding a welcome at Kara and Olivia, who returned it with a cool smile. 'Not at all. Leo just wants to chew my ear about figures anyway. You've saved me.'

'Hmph,' Leo said good-naturedly. 'As if that would get me anywhere.'

There was general laughter as Ethan sat in the spare chair. It was between Leo and Kara and opposite Olivia, and he glanced at her as he sat down.

'Looking forward to tomorrow, Kara?' Ethan asked.

'You betcha.' She grinned.

Hearing her Aussie accent, Ethan realised the Brits were outnumbered at their table tonight.

'I don't think I'll be able to sleep. I feel like a kid on Christmas Eve.'

Leo laughed. 'That's what I like to see,' he said. 'Enthusiasm.'

Ethan smiled as he glanced at Declan, who was looking at Kara as if she was a tasty little Christmas treat waiting under the tree and he was Santa. Ethan felt a pang in the centre of his chest. He'd known that feeling.

He'd *loved* that feeling.

The feeling that you never wanted to be anywhere else, with anyone else, just wrapped up in a bubble, just the two of you.

'Don't worry, darlin',' Declan said, exaggerating his accent. 'I have just the thing for insomnia.'

Everyone laughed, but still Ethan felt the pang throb a little harder. Leo had the same look as Declan and they were both clearly very contented men. Satisfaction oozed from their pores.

He glanced at Olivia again. Had she ever had anyone special? He realised he'd been so busy these past five days keeping his distance that he hadn't bothered to find out much about her life that didn't relate to work. There was ten years lost between them—maybe the wariness he saw in her expression now was to do with a man?

Conversation naturally flowed onto the case for a while, and it was good seeing Olivia relax again. She was in her comfort zone and the old spark came back. The passion and the fervour she obviously had for what she was doing sent a little buzz around the group and it was hard not to get a little high off it.

Ethan knew that feeling well. He'd got the same kick from the work he'd done these past ten years. Sure, initially when he'd first joined the army it had been the pressure and the danger he'd thrived on. The risks of front line work had made him feel more alive than he'd ever felt back home, with a drunken father and a stiflingly over-protective brother.

But he'd learned the hard way the downside of front line work. That you couldn't save everyone and that innocent people too often paid the price.

Leo had thought Ethan had joined up to spite him, and in some ways he had. But he'd caught the bug—the thrill of transforming somebody's life. And that was why he did it.

'You're sticking around for the hospital ball?' Kara asked Olivia, dragging Ethan back into the conversation.

Olivia shrugged. 'Oh… I…I didn't know there *was* a ball.'

Kara frowned at Ethan and Leo. 'What's the matter with you two?' She tsked with a smile on her face. 'You're really not very good hosts, are you?' She looked back at Olivia. 'It's the Lighthouse Ball—it's the highlight of the year. It's on in two weeks. *Everyone* goes.'

Olivia stilled with what she hoped was a smile on her face. Oh. *That* ball. Memories swamped her. A fabulous red dress. An exquisite set of matching lingerie. She'd been to *that* ball a decade ago—on Ethan's arm.

'You will come, right?' Kara said. 'Don't make me be the only Aussie there.'

Olivia shook her head. *Been there, done that.* 'I don't know how Ama will be by then.'

'No, Kara's right. It was remiss of me not to mention it,' Leo interjected. 'You should definitely go.' He looked at his watch. 'You should get Ethan to take you. You remember how much Ethan loves to dance, right?'

Leo grinned at his brother, and if Olivia hadn't been so annoyed at Leo she'd have been heartened by how much closer the two men were now, compared to their toxic relationship a decade ago.

'Funny,' Ethan said to his brother. 'You're hysterical.' He looked at Kara. 'I don't dance,' he said.

Olivia nearly snorted at the understatement. He could manage a waltz/shuffle and that was about it. He much preferred to mingle and be charming and to look dashing in a tux and turn every woman's head.

The last thing she wanted to do was go to a damn hospital ball with Ethan.

Ethan in a tux.

She'd had a fantasy about him in a tux involving a scalpel as well.

'Sorry—got to go, guys,' Leo said. 'Lizzie can barely stay up past nine these days.'

'And to think,' Ethan quipped, 'he used to party with princesses till dawn.'

Leo grinned at his brother. 'Totally overrated,' he said, then departed quickly.

Olivia saw Leo's departure as a perfect opportunity to effect her own, but before she could get her goodbyes out Kara was back onto the subject of the ball.

'Are you sure about the ball?'

Olivia nodded quickly. 'I don't have a dress anyway,' she said, hoping that another woman would understand such a conundrum even if it was hogwash.

'Oh, good grief, that's not a problem,' Kara dismissed with a wave of her hand. 'Have you *been* to Oxford Street? With your figure we could find you something in a jiffy. Plenty of places in London to shop for ballgowns. Actually, I even know this great place where you can get some Australian designer stuff.' She paused for a second and narrowed her eyes as she stared at a spot just above Olivia's head. 'You're from Sydney, you said, right?'

Olivia nodded. 'Ah…yes. But my parents were flying doctors so I mainly grew up in the Outback. Not many ball frocks out there,' she said, trying to make a joke.

But Kara was clearly enthused about the idea.

Ethan could see Olivia's lack of enthusiasm a mile away. 'Kara,' he said with mock sternness, 'you're badgering.'

'Sorry,' Kara said, but her grin didn't look very contrite to Ethan and his spine prickled—in a bad way—when she looked speculatively from him to Olivia and then back to him again.

'You just never know, right?' Kara said. 'The craziest things happen at balls,' she murmured, and she slid her hand onto Declan's and they smiled at each other.

Ethan suppressed an eye-roll. He'd already heard from Lizzie about how Declan and Kara had set tongues wagging at the Princess Catherine's ball because of a saucy stolen kiss. Why was it that people in love thought everyone else should be in love too?

They were worse than reformed smokers.

'Come on, love,' Declan said, standing. 'I think it's time we go before you're whipping out the tape measure. And you've got a big day tomorrow.'

Olivia was relieved when Kara took the bait. With them gone she'd have the perfect excuse to be gone too.

'Well, let me know if you change your mind about the ball,' Kara said as she shrugged into the jacket that had been slung around the back of her chair. 'Or the dress shopping.'

Olivia nodded, relieved that talk of the ball would soon be over. 'I will,' she said with absolutely no intention of following through.

The couple turned to leave, but at the last moment Kara stopped and turned back mid-collar-straightening.

'Oh, God,' she said, looking at Olivia. 'I just realised... *Olivia Fairchild...* Your parents were the flying doctors that were killed a few years back in that terrible bushfire, right? I'm so, *so* sorry...that was such a tragedy.'

Olivia blinked as a hot spike of pain cleaved her right through the middle. So far away from home and five years down the track she hadn't expected anyone to get the association, and even though Kara was an Australian it was completely unexpected.

'Oh…yes,' she said, forcing the words out around a throat that felt as if it was collapsing in on itself. 'Thank you,' she stammered. 'It was a…shock.'

'It was awful,' Kara agreed. 'Just awful.'

'Yes,' Olivia said, nodding automatically, her head roaring with a tsunami of suppressed emotions.

Ethan looked from Olivia to Kara and then back to Olivia again. Olivia looked like she'd been struck, her peaches and cream complexion almost waxy now it was so pale. He frowned. *What the hell…?*

Olivia's parents were dead?

Ethan glanced at Kara, who clearly realised she'd spoken without thinking and didn't know what to say next. She looked at him, lost, and then shrugged, a panicked *help me* look on her face.

He nodded his head at her. 'It's okay,' he murmured. 'Go home and get some sleep. We need your A Game tomorrow.'

Declan nodded at Ethan over Kara's head. 'C'mon, darlin',' he said, and Ethan was relieved when the couple quietly withdrew.

Olivia sat staring at the glass of wine she'd barely touched and Ethan wished he knew where—*how*—to start. Olivia had been so close to her parents. He remembered what a foreign concept that had been for him and how they'd both struggled to understand the dynamics of each other's families when they were used to different upbringings.

'I'm sorry,' he said.

Olivia shut her eyes. She didn't want to hear his condolences. She didn't want to share such a terrible gut-wrenching part of her life with him. It was too…*significant*—something lovers shared—and at the moment she could barely breathe from the sense of loss weighing down her lungs and settling in her bones.

She'd forgotten how much it hurt. How much she missed them. Being overseas, being away from it all, it was easy to forget it had happened. Easy to pretend she'd go home and they'd be waiting for her.

Sometimes the stark reality that she'd *never* see them again—which played like a soft chant in the back of her head anyway—roared out at her and hit her like a blast wave to the chest.

'It's fine,' she said, her thumb rubbing absently over the cool fiery opal in her ring, remembering the day her parents had given it to her.

'It's *not* fine, Olivia,' he dismissed tersely, then frowned at her, trying to understand. 'Why didn't you tell me?'

Olivia glared at him. 'Oh, you're annoyed because I didn't *tell* you?'

Ethan sighed. 'No, Olivia. No. I just…I wish I'd known.'

Olivia clung to the slow burn of anger in her chest. It was easier to be mad at him than at two dead people, than at an act of nature that had killed fifteen others that day.

She sucked in a breath as a wave of pain crested in her throat. 'You could have *asked*.'

Ethan blinked at the low accusation in her voice, trying to think back to the conversations they'd had since she'd returned. It was true they

hadn't really talked about anything personal—
hadn't he only just thought that tonight?—but…

'You said your parents had given you the
money for your charity.'

Olivia snorted. 'They did,' she said bitterly.
'In their will.'

Ethan was silenced by the depth of her grief.
He'd lost his father a decade ago, his mother
ten years before that. And despite finding out
about his mother's infidelities after her death,
and his contentious relationship with his father—
or maybe because of them—his loss and grief
had been compounded.

But that had been a long time ago.

Aaliyah's death, on the other hand, had not.
And, whether Olivia knew it or not, he understood the rawness of grief. He also understood
now that *this* was what her reserve was about.

She was hurting.

She was grieving.

'What happened?'

Olivia felt a hot tear well in her eye and fall
down her cheek and she brushed it savagely
away. She knew he wasn't going to let it go—

best to just get it out there as quickly and pain-lessly as possible.

'Five years ago…a massive bushfire…it swept through Outback Queensland. We were all there. Mum and Dad were pitching in with the author-ities, out driving a rusty old four-wheel drive somebody had commandeered for them, help-ing to evacuate all the outlying properties, giv-ing first aid, et cetera.'

Olivia could still smell the thick smoke blan-keting the air, feel the sting of her eyes and the irritation of her airways, hear the almighty roar of the fire as the wind swept it along at a horri-fying pace.

She picked up her glass of wine and stared at the fluid level as she absently swirled it. 'I was in the rural hospital, dealing with the casual-ties as they came in. I'd wanted to go with them but they said I was needed at the hospital. And I was, of course.'

Another tear fell and she dashed it away too.

'I'd just finished organising an evac for my third escharotomy of the day when the police came. The wind had changed…they'd been cut off…surrounded…'

Olivia shut her eyes, trying to block out the demons that had dogged her for so long.

'I dreamt about how they must have died for months afterwards. How *terrifying* it must have been. How terrified *they* must have been… I know they would have been thinking about me… worried about me…'

Ethan sucked in a slow ragged breath. He could tell her the smoke would have rendered them unconscious first. He could say it would have been quick—so quick. Those fires moved at a horrendous pace.

But she knew all that. She was a doctor. Except when she shut her eyes.

Then she was a daughter.

'I'm sorry,' he said again.

Olivia opened her eyes. She didn't want him to be sorry. She wanted them back. But Ethan couldn't do that. Nobody could. And she was damned if she was going to vent her spleen to a guy with shadows in his eyes who had rebutted every effort she'd ever made to get him to open up to her.

She shrugged, clawing back her composure. Reaching for the reserve she wore now like an armour against the things that threatened to cut her off at the knees.

'I guess that goes in the *bad luck* basket, huh?' she said, her voice still husky with emotion as she raised her glass in his direction.

Ethan's gut clenched at her faux flippancy. 'Olivia… Don't… You can talk to me…'

'No, Ethan. You and I…we *don't* talk.'

'Maybe we should.'

Olivia snorted. *Like that's going to be a two-way street.* 'Okay, then,' she said, her voice heavy with sarcasm. 'You go first. Tell me, Ethan…' she leaned in closer to him '…what happened to you while you were in the military that made you even more screwed up than before you left?'

Ethan shook his head. 'Olivia—'

'Bum-*bah*!' Olivia hoped that sounded like a game show buzzer. 'Wrong answer.'

'Olivia.'

She ignored the note of warning in his voice.

She was riding a surge of anger that she thought had been resolved a long time ago.

*Obviously not.*

'Oh, no, Ethan. *No, no, no.* You don't get to hear *my* sob story and then just stay all stoic and clammed up. You don't get to have all of *me* and keep all of *you* to yourself like last time. That got me burned bad.' Olivia gave an hysterical little laugh at the irony of her word-choice.

*Burned.*

'You want me to talk to you? Well, that's a two-way street and we both know...' she paused and threw back her wine in three long swallows '... that's not the way you play the game.'

Then she placed the glass on the table and stood. 'I'm going to check in on Ama before I go home. I'll see you tomorrow.'

Ethan stood too. 'I'll come with you.'

Olivia glared at him. 'No,' she said. 'You will *not.*'

# CHAPTER SEVEN

ETHAN STOOD IN the corridor just outside Theatre Nine the next morning, watching Kara and Olivia scrubbing up through the glass window in the swing door that led into the scrub room from outside.

They were chatting—not that he could hear what they were talking about. He wondered if it was about Kara's revelation last night. About Olivia's parents. Or maybe about the ball again.

Although he doubted it. If he knew Olivia it would be about Ama, about the surgery. She liked to go over the game plan as she scrubbed. He'd forgotten that about her, but working with her on his recent surgeries had brought it all back. She'd want to be focused on today, on the surgery. She'd be going over and over the plan in her head.

The last thing she'd want was to be in a bad

emotional place. She was going to need all her concentration for today and she wouldn't want to have any distractions.

He admired that about her, and working side by side with her these past few days he'd been impressed by what a first-class surgeon Olivia had become. He'd always known she would be—she'd been impressive a decade ago, when her surgical skills were in their infancy—but he was pleased to see that his predictions had come to fruition.

Pleased that he'd had the opportunity to see her in action again.

Pleased that nothing seemed to faze her.

Her front line experience had shaped her into a mighty fine surgical all-rounder, as it had him, and no matter what surgery he was doing she'd scrubbed up and joined the fray, Ama's schedule permitting.

'Excuse me,' someone said from behind him.

'Sorry,' Ethan said, stepping aside as one of the scout nurses carrying a sterile tray of instruments pushed open the swing door and entered.

Ethan felt his muscles ache slightly at the sudden movement. After Olivia's news he hadn't got much sleep last night, and he'd hit his home gym around midnight, hoping to cause enough exhaustion to cure his insomnia.

It had been that or the bottle.

He'd been working on his physio every night since he'd begun spending his days working side by side with Olivia. He'd been suffering from a restless energy when he got home each night and it helped.

He'd always welcomed the quiet of his apartment, but it seemed oppressively so after a day with chatty Olivia. She seemed always to be in his head, and alone with his own thoughts— thoughts that usually involved Aaliyah—he'd been desperate for something to drive her out.

So he'd been exercising. Hard to think of anything other than pain when he had to push himself through. Still, he was already feeling the benefits in the strength and stamina of his quads.

And it was a much better option than what he would have chosen not that long ago—liquid denial.

Kara and Olivia finished up their scrub and headed for the Theatre, arms out in front of them. Ethan quickly pushed open the door and stepped into the scrub room.

'Olivia,' he said, and both women stopped and turned around to look at him. 'Can I have a moment, please?'

Olivia stifled a sigh. She'd thought it would be too much to ask to just get through this day without some kind of post-mortem over last night. Kara had already apologised three times during their scrub.

Olivia turned her head and smiled at Kara. 'Go on ahead,' she assured the junior surgeon. 'I won't be a moment.' When Kara was gone she turned back to Ethan. 'I don't want to do this now, okay?'

Ethan nodded. He'd suspected as much, but he didn't want her going in there with any kind of unspoken stuff between them—they needed to be a team. Best to clear the air now. 'I just wanted to—'

'I know what you "just wanted to," Ethan,' Olivia interrupted impatiently. 'But not now, okay? Can we just get through Ama's surgery? Can today please just be about Ama?'

Ethan shoved his hands on his hips. Clearly she was in the zone and *did not* want to be yanked out of it. 'Okay.'

Olivia nodded. 'Good. See you in there.'

The surgery was involved. They began with removing the protruding teeth that had been warped and buckled by disease, then they cut away all the old scar tissue. Bone was harvested from Ama's hip to replace the missing section of maxilla and plated and screwed into place. Then a thick piece of skin was removed from her arm and used as a graft to cover the gaping hole in Ama's face.

Such a large piece of grafted skin required a blood supply, so they used a small artery and vein from the neck to provide this. Lastly they were able to rebuild the mouth, using what Ama already had and reshaping it to the way it had been before she'd fallen victim to NOMA.

Five hours later Ama's face was finally whole again. The surgery was done and she was on her way to the High Dependency ward, where she would be closely monitored for the first twenty-four to forty-eight hours.

'That was incredible,' Kara said, her eyes sparkling as she degowned and tossed it in the bin.

Olivia nodded, relieved and very happy with the result. 'Yes.' She grinned. 'It was.'

Ama's face would always be different from everyone else's. Her cheek would look a different colour and consistency to the rest of her face, with an obvious demarcation around the graft, and her lip line would always be just a little bit deviated.

But she'd be able to swallow, eat, chew and talk properly. And, more important, she'd have a more socially acceptable face. She could go to school. She could make friends and play with the other children.

She could be a *child*.

'You guys were awesome,' Kara continued as she and Olivia headed to the change-room.

Olivia wanted to get up to the HDU as soon as possible—Ethan had gone with Ama.

'You didn't even really talk to each other

but you both seemed to know what each other needed. It was like you'd been operating together for years!'

Olivia had been so engrossed, so in the zone, she hadn't really noticed. But, looking back, she realised Kara was right. She and Ethan had worked together like a well-oiled machine. But then they'd always been very compatible—in *every* way.

'It's just practice,' Olivia dismissed. 'You do this for long enough and it becomes second nature.'

'Well, you call it what you want,' Kara said as she pushed open the change-room doors. 'I call it synchronicity. And it was pure magic to be a part of it, so thank you.'

Olivia didn't know what to say to that. Everything had gone very smoothly—no rabbits out of hats required. 'You weren't so shabby yourself,' she said.

Kara blushed and looked at Olivia, her face glowing from the compliment. 'Really?'

Olivia laughed. 'Yes, really. Now, stop fishing

for compliments and let me get dressed so I can go see our patient.'

Kara gave a cheeky salute. 'Yes, ma'am.'

But she left Olivia in peace and Olivia was dressed and heading to the HDU in ten minutes.

The first couple of hours post-op Ama was pretty out of it. Olivia, Ril and Dali sat quietly by her side, talking occasionally but essentially maintaining a silent vigil. Ethan checked on her a couple of times, with Olivia assuring him that she'd page him when Ama woke or if any complications occurred.

It was in the third hour that things started to go wrong. Ama awoke in a great deal of distress and pain. She was clearly frightened and thrashing around the bed, pulling off her oxygen mask, calling for her mother.

She was given a bolus of painkiller intravenously and her morphine infusion rate was increased. It worked temporarily, but she became more agitated and distressed again over the next hour—crying and at one stage, before Olivia leapt up to stop her, clawing at her face, blindly beating at it.

Ril was becoming distressed by her daughter's condition as more pain relief was given, the infusion increased further and some sedation added in on top. And both Ethan and Olivia were worried she would damage some of the reconstructive work they'd done with all her thrashing around. They were particularly worried about the viability of the graft. They checked beneath the dressings, but whilst it was oozing there didn't seem to be any excessive blood and the graft still appeared intact.

Nonetheless neither of them wanted to take a chance, and Ethan ordered arm restraints which wouldn't allow Ama to bend her elbows. A nurse wrapped them around her arms and Olivia felt better knowing that Ama wouldn't be able to reach her face any more if she remained unsettled.

When next Ama woke she was talking gibberish.

'I don't know what she's saying,' Dali said to Olivia, and there was fear in her eyes for her young charge. 'They're just words that don't make sense and then she talks crazy stuff about spiders on the ceiling.'

Both Ethan and Olivia looked at each other. 'It's the morphine,' she said.

Ethan nodded. Of course he should have thought about the possibility of Ama reacting badly to the morphine—the spider hallucinations were a clear sign of that—but the language barrier made everything so much harder.

'We'll change it to another opioid.'

A different infusion was started, and a bolus of it given, but Ama was in a significant state so was started on an infusion of a drug to keep her sedated, which finally managed to settle her completely after another half an hour.

By early evening she was sleeping heavily, although responding briskly to stimuli, and everyone was exhausted. Ril had fallen asleep in a hard plastic chair beside the bed, holding her daughter's hand, her head on the mattress at an awkward angle. Dali was also dozing.

Olivia looked at the monitor. All Ama's vitals looked in good shape and the oxygen mask was firmly in situ. The figures blurred before her eyes as she felt her eyelids drooping. It had been a long and exhausting day. After the smoothness and success of the surgery none of them had planned for this kind of stormy post-op course, although things like reactions to opioids weren't uncommon.

It had been draining. And awful to see such genuine distress and terror in Ama, who was usually so bright and sunny despite all the reasons for her not to be.

Add to that the tumultuous events of last night that had led to very little sleep, and Olivia was finding it hard to keep her eyes open. The room was so quiet and the steady *beep, beep, beep* of Ama's monitor was strangely hypnotic. Despite the hard plastic of the chair she was sitting in, it was bliss to shut her eyes. Just for a moment.

Olivia wasn't sure how long had elapsed when the trilling of Ama's monitor woke her. She was disorientated at first as she looked at her watch— almost 10:00 p.m. Her back and neck protested as she squinted to focus on the monitor and identify the alarm in the darkened cubicle.

The oxygen saturations had fallen into the eighties. She also noted there was some tachycardia, and Ama's blood pressure was a little on the lower end—but it had been anyway, since the sedation had begun.

Olivia stood up and went over to Ama's bedside. The oxygen mask had slipped off. She went to place it back on but her hand stilled when she noticed the pallor of Ama's lips and the gurgly sound of her breathing.

'Ama?' Olivia said, reaching for the girl's hand to give it a squeeze. The hand was cold and clammy. Olivia frowned as she placed the mask and called, 'Ama!' again, giving her the firm shake of the shoulder to which she'd responded briskly just over an hour ago—nothing.

Ama's nurse arrived. 'The ICU registrar is a couple of minutes away,' she said. 'Ama's been getting increasingly tachycardic the past fifteen minutes, and her sats are starting to drift, so I want him to check her out.'

Olivia nodded, pleased the nurse was on the ball. 'Can you page Ethan too, please?' she asked.

The nurse went off to do Olivia's bidding. Ama's saturations had barely improved, so Olivia turned the oxygen up.

'Ama?' Olivia said, applying a painful stimulus to the girl's sternum, using the knuckle of her index finger and rubbing hard. Still nothing. Olivia reached over and paused the infusion of sedation, which she noticed had been decreased significantly since she'd drifted off to sleep.

Ama should be responding.

The tone of the saturation trace dropped and Olivia glanced up to see they were only eighty per cent now, despite the extra oxygen.

She also noticed the respiratory trace was slowing right down. A very bad feeling welled in the pit of Olivia's stomach as she flicked on the light and assessed the movement of Ama's chest. It seemed to be barely moving at all.

Ril woke up, blinking as bright light flooded the cubicle. So did Dali. They were speaking to each other in their language, and Dali was asking Olivia questions, but Olivia was back at the ABCs of medicine.

*Airway.*

That was always priority number one in medicine, and Olivia was beginning to think Ama's was compromised. The gurgling she could hear was a concern, and Olivia leaned down, her ear to Ama's mouth, as she used her index finger to give Ama some jaw-thrust. Blood welled out of Ama's mouth and Ril looked horrified, pointing and crying and talking rapidly to Dali.

'What is wrong, Olivia?' Dali asked. 'What is wrong?'

Now Olivia was certain Ama was bleeding, but had no idea to what extent.

The feeling of foreboding increased.

'I'm not sure,' she said, reaching for the Yankaeur sucker jammed under the pillow, 'but Ethan's coming and we're going to take good care of her—do you hear? Please take Ril along to the parents' lounge and I'll come and explain everything as soon as I can.'

Olivia had a feeling this was going to get

messy. And the thick blood slurping noisily into the tubing from Ama's mouth confirmed it.

Olivia was aware on a peripheral level that Dali and Ril were having a heated exchange but she shut it out. Ama was her concern.

*Come on, little girl. Don't do this.*

*Do not do this.*

'Dali,' Olivia said as the blood kept coming and Ama remained unresponsive, despite the very potent stimulus of a large plastic sucker hitting the back of her throat, 'get her out of here *now!*'

The nurse returned as Dali led a wailing Ril away. 'She needs a twenty mil per kilo bolus of whatever you have running,' Olivia said. 'And get some of her blood from the fridge.'

They'd cross-matched six units for surgery but had only used one during the operation because the blood loss had been so minimal.

Ama was making up for it now.

Two more nurses entered the cubicle area as the registrar arrived. And Ethan about thirty seconds later. She'd never been more pleased to see him. She was aware that she was quaking on the inside but her training was taking over. Later she'd probably throw up, but right now she was in the zone.

'She's bleeding,' Olivia said, not looking up from Ama.

Ethan felt the same surge of adrenaline he always felt when an emergency evolved. He used it to his advantage to focus himself, to hone his intuition.

'Let me look,' he said, striding over to where Olivia stood. 'Pull the bed out.'

One of the nurses released the brakes on the bed and moved the bed down so Ethan could slip in at the head of the bed. He angled an unresponsive Ama's jaw open and could see nothing for the blood.

The alarm behind him trilled again as Ama's heart-rate started to fall.

'Get the resus trolley,' Olivia told one of the nurses as she watched the alarming drop of Ama's heart-rate on the monitor.

'I need a laryngoscope,' Ethan said.

Within seconds they had both. Ethan tried to look down her throat using the laryngoscope but his view was totally obscured by congealed blood. He pulled out.

'Get me a trache kit,' he said.

One of the nurses scurried off to get one as the other two busied themselves drawing up resus drugs. When Ama's heart-rate hit fifty Olivia started external compressions and asked for atropine to be administered.

The nurse who had fetched the sterile trache pack opened it for Ethan and opened a sterile pair of gloves for him.

'Page Jock,' Ethan said as he plunged his left hand into the left glove, preparing to do a down-and-dirty emergency tracheostomy. Securing Ama's airway was vital. 'Tell him to get his butt back in here. As soon as this trache is done we're going back to Theatre to get the bleeder.'

The nurse squirted Betadine over Ama's throat as someone else laid the back of the bed flat, then raised the bed higher to accommodate Ethan's six-foot-two frame. The atropine had done the trick and Olivia had stopped compressions for the moment. She also asked for a pair of gloves, knowing that Ethan might need a hand, leaving the registrar to monitor everything else.

Ethan made a quick incision into Ama's throat, his plan being to secure the airway by the insertion of a tracheostomy tube and get to Theatre ASAP. But when he opened the neck there was so much blood it took him longer than he'd hoped, and he and Olivia literally had to scoop out the congealed blood to identify where he was going to stick the tube, all the while conscious of the screaming alarms and the ticking of the clock.

He finally placed it after two fraught minutes, and it was a relief when Olivia squeezed in the first breath via the bloodied Laerdel bag and there was immediate chest movement and improvement of the oxygen saturations.

Ethan glanced at Olivia. She had blood on her clothes but her look of sheer relief was exactly the way he felt—as if they were back in the field and they'd executed a major save together. For a moment he'd never felt closer to her.

'Let's get her to Theatre,' Ethan said.

Olivia nodded. 'I'll have a quick chat to Ril and join you.'

* * *

By midnight Ama was out of Theatre and had been taken to ICU this time. They'd identified the bleeding—most probably caused by Ama's initial thrashing around—and she was going to be kept ventilated and sedated overnight and hopefully have the tracheostomy removed in the next few days.

By the time they'd seen her settled in the unit and spoken to Ril and Dali it was close to one in the morning and Olivia was dead on her feet.

'C'mon,' Ethan said to her as she hovered around Ama's bedside. 'Home for you.'

Olivia shook her head. 'I want to stay.'

'You're exhausted,' Ethan said, pulling her to one side. 'You need a break.'

'I'll catch some sleep in a spare office somewhere later,' she dismissed.

'Olivia.'

'I'm fine,' she reiterated, looking over his shoulder at the monitor.

'Olivia…' Ethan said again.

Olivia dragged her gaze off the monitor to

look at him—his tone had brooked no argument. *'I'm fine.'*

'You are not fine,' he said. 'You are running on empty. You need to get out of those clothes, which have blood on them. You need a shower. When did you last eat? You need food. And you need to sleep—a *decent* sleep on a decent bed, not some awful office examination couch.'

Olivia looked down at her clothes, realising for the first time that they had a patch of dried blood which looked as if someone had dabbed her with a large paintbrush dipped in red paint. Ethan was still in his Theatre garb.

'I'll get some scrubs,' she murmured.

'Liv…' Ethan shut his eyes, cursing to himself as the word he shouldn't use slipped out. *Damn it.* He was too tired to care. 'She's stable now, and sedated. At least go home, have a shower, change your clothes, have something to eat.'

Olivia didn't even register that he'd called her Liv. At least not on a conscious level. Having a shower and something to eat sounded like bliss—she was starving. All she'd had to eat since breakfast was a packet of crisps from the vending machine. But she was staying a twenty-minute cab-ride away from the hospital and she wanted to be close while Ama was still in ICU.

Olivia shook her head. 'I can't,' she said.

Now the drama was over she was starting to feel a little shaky. She'd been so terrified they were going to lose Ama at one stage.

'I talked them into this. I told them we could fix her. I promised Ril she would be okay...'

'Olivia, she *is* okay.' Ethan put his hands on her shoulders and waited until she was looking at him. 'Listen to me,' he said. 'This isn't your fault. This isn't my fault. Bad things happen sometimes and post-op haemorrhage is always a risk—you know that. And there was a combination of factors here. But she's fine. You did good.'

Olivia saw the flecks in his eyes flare to life with the conviction of his words. She knew he was right, but a combination of adrenaline over-load and low blood sugar were clouding her judgement. '*We* did good,' she said.

Ethan smiled. 'Yes. We did. Now...' He squeezed

her shoulders gently before dropping his hands. 'Go home.'

Olivia shook her head. 'I'll just go to the Theatre change-rooms and have a shower. I'll get something from a vending machine.'

'No, Olivia. You need to get out of here for a while. Clear your head. Get some distance. This case has taken up your whole life for weeks and weeks now.'

'I'll be too far away,' Olivia said, starting to get a little fed up with his persistence now. 'I don't want to go too far.'

Ethan stared in exasperation at her. 'Fine— come to my place, then. I'm heading there and it's only a five-minute walk. You can shower, change, eat and then if you really insist on coming back I'll walk you.'

Olivia chewed her lip, undecided. She desperately wanted a shower and something to eat. Sleep she could live without. It was tempting. 'You're still in the same place?'

Ethan nodded. 'Yep. And Il Conte is still just down the road, and I have a takeaway container of their best spaghetti in my fridge.'

Olivia felt the flutter of her belly as a hundred great memories rushed out at her. How many more would be waiting for her at Ethan's place? She doubted there was a square inch, certainly not a single horizontal surface, they hadn't made love on.

But it *was* the perfect solution—a place close by for a quick pit stop and then off again.

In and out—no time for the memories to cling and hold.

*And there was a time she would have killed for Il Conte's spaghetti.*

'Okay,' she conceded. 'But I'm coming straight back.'

'Of course.'

'Let me just check on her one last time.'

'Okay. I'll get out of these and grab some fresh scrubs for you and meet you at the entrance in ten?'

Olivia nodded. And hoped to God she hadn't just made the biggest mistake of her life.

# CHAPTER EIGHT

IT TOOK OLIVIA ten seconds to realise she *had* just made the biggest mistake of her life. Stepping into Ethan's apartment was like entering a time warp where nothing had changed. The upstairs apartment of the old Victorian terrace was exactly the same and it was as if they were coming home from work together as they so often had, chatting about their day, anticipating a long session of lovemaking.

Even just standing inside the entranceway old memories floated around her, dizzying her with their potency.

*She really needed to eat something.*

Hell, she could recall a time when they'd fallen to the floor right where she was standing, so eager to get their hands on each other they hadn't been able to wait. The door had barely clicked shut, for crying out loud.

And…oh, God…the door—Ethan had pressed her against that once and brought her to a screaming orgasm in under a minute.

'Go have a shower,' Ethan said, brushing past her. 'I'll heat up the spaghetti.'

Olivia doubted her legs would carry her that far, afflicted as they were suddenly by a bad case of the shakes. Her head spun a little. 'Actually, do you mind if I eat first?' she asked. 'I think my blood sugar is bottoming out.'

Ethan turned. She looked pale and washed out. She swayed a little as he watched and he took a step towards her.

'Don't,' Olivia said as she reached for the nearby wall for stability.

If he touched her she'd melt right into him, and God alone knew where *that* would lead in this place where she'd spent about seventy-five per cent of her time in his bed. Or on his couch, or his table, or against his walls or his door…

'You look like you're about to fall over.'

'I won't,' she assured him, waving him back. 'As long as you feed me pronto.'

Ethan nodded. 'On it.'

Olivia followed him into the gleaming steel and granite kitchen at a slower pace and sat down at the big central black marble counter that hosted four bar stools. Her stomach grumbled and her hands shook as she placed them against the cool surface.

*Somewhere else they'd made love.*

Her brain shut down that memory before it even got out of the starting gate and she concentrated instead on Ethan, clattering around, putting a bowl in the microwave, piling another one with spaghetti, waiting to put it in. She noted the familiar Il Conte container, and how amazing the food smelled even cold, and she almost told him not to bother to heat it up she was *that* hungry.

'You want a coffee?' he asked. 'Probably be handy if you're going back.'

Olivia nodded. It was going to be a long night, and she was going to need all the help she could get. He turned to a fancy coffee machine that *was* new, placed a pod in the top and a cup under the spout and pressed a button. The microwave beeped and he pulled the bowl out, giving the spaghetti a stir with a fork. She watched steam rise off it and her mouth watered.

He went to return it to the microwave. 'It'll be fine like that,' she assured him.

Ethan frowned. 'It's not heated all the way through. It's only just warm, really.'

Olivia shook her head. 'Don't care,' she dismissed, holding her hand out for the bowl. 'Near enough is good enough.'

He chuckled as he passed it over. Her belly growled again and she wasn't entirely sure it was anything to do with food. His sexy stubble was even more so as he stood in his kitchen, serving her spaghetti and coffee as he'd done a hundred times before.

Olivia demolished the bowl in two minutes flat. She didn't lift her head, she didn't converse, she didn't notice when Ethan placed her coffee on the bench. She just ate, barely registering the aroma of basil and the sweet taste of fresh tomatoes.

When she was done she looked up, finding Ethan's amused gaze. 'Sorry.' She grimaced.

Ethan laughed as he cradled his coffee cup in

his hand. 'I always did enjoy watching you eat,' he murmured.

Olivia remembered all the other things he'd enjoyed watching her do. Laughing at a joke, slipping on a pair of high heels, shaving her legs.

Getting undressed.

Coming as if the world was going to end.

Her stomach growled again, and for damn sure this time it was *nothing* to do with food. He was watching her mouth and, nervous, she licked her lips, finding some stray sauce and removing it with her tongue.

Ethan almost groaned out loud as her nervous licking still managed to miss a bit of sauce. Once upon a time, standing here in his kitchen, with her sitting opposite in that chair, he'd have just leaned across the bench and licked it off. And the desire to do so now thrummed through his veins like a siren call.

He'd *never* wanted to taste her this badly.

Instead, exercising the control he'd perfected in the military, he ground his feet into the marble tiles, reached for a serviette from the counter behind him and passed it to her. 'You missed some.'

Olivia took it and dabbed at her mouth, excruciatingly aware of his intent stare. Of the way he'd paused, coffee cup halfway to his mouth, and just looked at her, taking in every movement. She knew that stare. It was stirring memories and stroking along her pelvic floor, causing the muscles there to preen in an utterly Pavlovian response.

Shower.

*Shower, shower, shower.*

Her brain was doing its best to drag her back from the edge. To remember how he'd used her, hurt her. She'd *made love* to him a hundred times in this apartment, fallen *in love* with him, and all the while he'd just been *having sex* with the woman his brother had wanted.

'I think you're done,' he murmured.

His voice blew over her, soft as feathers. Caressing her skin and tickling a memory of the past out of hiding.

The time he'd tied her wrists and ankles to his bed and spent hours taunting her, touching her spread-eagled body, tracing his tongue all over her. Backing off every time she built, refusing to let her come, gorging himself instead on his tactile feast and driving her mad with lust until finally he'd relented.

*'I think you're done,'* he'd said.

And when he'd put his mouth to her she'd had an orgasm that had gone on for an eternity.

Her blood flowed slow and thick through her veins as the memory played out. It pounded through her head and washed through her ears. Her breath felt like syrup in her lungs. Her abdominals had turned to goo, like flaming marshmallow, melting her to the chair.

Olivia saw Ethan's knuckles whiten as his grip on the cup increased. Was he thinking about it too?

Ethan wasn't sure which memory Olivia was caught up in, but she needed to stop now if she wanted to leave here unmolested. Today had been intense—very intense. It would be bad to do something neither of them should just because they were reacting to the pressure of the day and a bunch of memories.

Even if they *were* really great memories.

She was looking at him as if she wanted to

hurdle the bench and drag him to the ground. But she wouldn't thank him for it in the morning. He knew her too well.

'Olivia.'

Olivia blinked at the warning in his voice, the memory receding as awareness of the present filtered back in. A well of loathing rose in her chest and burned hard and high in her throat.

*Ama.*

She had to get back to Ama.

Olivia reached for her coffee cup and took a fortifying sip, too embarrassed even to look at Ethan. She took another and, as it wasn't too hot, blew on it and took a bigger swig. Then she placed it on the bench and stood.

'I'll have a shower and get out of your hair,' she said, still not looking at him.

Ethan didn't want her to go. Actually…he did. He wasn't sure he could last a night with her here in his apartment again and not just give in to what his body wanted. He'd felt dead inside for a year, but ten days back in her company and certain parts of him were very definitely coming back to life.

But she needed to sleep and that was more important. Maybe he could convince her after her shower?

'Scrubs on the back of the couch,' he said.

She didn't answer, didn't even acknowledge his words, just grabbed the scrubs on her way past and disappeared from his sight.

It was bliss under the hard, hot spray and Olivia wanted nothing more than to slide down the wall, hug her legs to her chest and nod off under the steady cleansing heat, until the tension in her muscles had eased and the squall inside her stomach had settled.

But she was afraid to shut her eyes. The whole shower smelled like him, smelled so male—soap and shampoo and aftershave—and she was reminded of how often they'd made love in here too.

A lot.

And Olivia knew the second she allowed her eyelids to shut she'd be there again, her back to the tiles, Ethan buried inside her, groaning *'Liv...'* into her ear as he came.

Or going down on her, looking totally in control despite his position of supplication on his knees in front of her, his hands holding onto the backs of her thighs, holding her up, as her world splintered around her.

Olivia ruthlessly shut off the taps as steam built in the cubicle, heating the mix of male aromas to a wild liquid cloud, painting her body, marinating her in memories. Drifting her into dangerous territory.

*Ama.*

She had to get back to Ama.

She towelled off quickly, throwing on her scrubs *sans* underwear—she'd sling her duffle coat on over the top and no one would ever know she was going commando. The aroma of fresh laundry and Ethan's spicy soap surrounded her, reminding her of clean sheets and him, and she yawned, her eyes gritty despite the shower.

She turned off the heating lamps and stepped out of the en-suite bathroom into Ethan's darkened bedroom. A shaft of light from the hallway penetrated into the gloom, lifting the visibility level a little. Enough to make out objects like his big soft bed—still in the same spot—beckoning her like a fluffy freaking cloud, with its blizzard-white duvet and matching pillows—something that had always seemed so out of place in this overwhelmingly male bachelor pad.

It whispered to her. *Rest. Sleep. Dream.*

And the thought of getting just a couple of hours' shut-eye was utterly, utterly seductive. But she dragged herself back from it, padding through his bedroom in her bare feet, the thick rug luxurious on her soles as she headed for her bag and coat and a brisk walk in the cold London night.

Then an object sitting on a shelf near the door caught her eye and she stopped. It looked eerily familiar, and despite her brain telling her she needed to get the hell out of his room she was drawn to it by the insistent tug of ancient strings.

Its shape became more distinct as she neared and Olivia's heart beat a solid tattoo in her chest as she reached for it. The bronze was cool as she wrapped her fingers around the miniature figurine, but the spark of memory soon heated the object, sending warm tingles up her arm.

*He'd kept it.*

Stupid tears needled at her eyeballs as she looked down at the nude young woman reclined in a pensive pose and she blinked them back. He probably didn't realise he still had it. Which fitted right in with the rest of the decade-old stuff in this apartment that time forgot.

He'd bought it at Portobello Road market because he'd said the woman's secretive smile reminded him of her just after she came. As if she'd touched the stars and knew all their secrets. That had been two days before she'd found out about his dastardly behaviour. Two blissful days when she'd floated on cloud nine because this exquisite, dainty, perfectly detailed piece of eighteenth-century sculpture had reminded him of her and the magic they made together.

Olivia ran her thumb over that Mona Lisa smile, remembering that day. It was probably the last time she'd ever been deep-down-in-her-bones happy.

'She's still beautiful, isn't she?'

Olivia's thumb stilled. She was aware suddenly of the heat of him at her back. Of his overwhelming presence enveloping her in a cloud of old memories and new desires. It fluttered in her pulse and prickled along her nerve-endings, peaking her nipples and fanning along the bare skin of her nape—her hair was up to avoid getting wet.

'Yes,' Olivia said, placing her gently back.

Ethan wanted to bury his nose in the exposed stretch of skin in front of him, right where her nape joined her shoulder, which the square neckline of the scrub shirt left beautifully exposed. He wanted to sniff her there. Inhale deeply. Smell his soap on her.

Remember back to the days when his smell used to be stamped all over her.

He itched to pull her hair out of its rough and ready up-do. The wet ends of the tendrils that had half fallen down taunted him more.

'I *am* sorry about what I did, Olivia.'

Olivia shut her eyes briefly. 'I know,' she said.

'It wasn't all mercenary. I did care for you too.'

'I know,' she repeated, then she took a deep

steady breath and opened her eyes as she turned to face him.

But he was close, so much closer than she'd realised, and his scent was intoxicating, and his neck was just there, its fat pulse bordering the hard ridge of his trachea, pounding right in front of her even through the thick growth of stubble.

She shut her eyes again as a wave of longing rolled through her, sweet and hot, like sherbet and crack cocaine.

She remembered how hard he'd fought for Ama tonight. How he'd taken over, securing her airway, fighting for the little girl's life. Scooping out blood, never giving up as he'd raced against the clock and the hazards of prolonged hypoxia.

'Thank you,' she said, her voice husky even to her own ears, thick and lumpy in her throat. 'For Ama.'

Ethan shook his head. She was looking at him with *those* eyes. Eyes frank with professional admiration and personal gratitude. A truly deadly combination. *Oh, crap.*

'Liv...'

And that was it for Olivia. A husky entreaty

so masculine but so needy. She couldn't fight it any more. She couldn't deny it any more. She and Ethan had been on a slow trajectory towards each other since coming back in contact again and tonight he had sling-shotted into her orbit in a most spectacular fashion.

She was lost. Heat and lust clouded her senses until her head was full of him. Every breath filled her up a little bit more until she was drowning in the essence of him. The intelligence of what she was about to do was so far out of her reach her brain might as well have been residing in Australia.

'Oh, God…Ethan,' she muttered as she slid her arm up to his neck and yanked him closer until her body was flush with his, going up on tippy-toe, shoulder to shoulder, hip to hip, feeling the hard press of him against her belly.

The golden flecks in his eyes were glowing the way they used to, with passion and life, and she had no hope now of resisting him now the shadows that had warned her to keep away were gone.

'I can't not do this.'

And then she pressed her mouth to his and she was lost in a vortex of arousal so strong there was no room for thought or for second-guessing. It was just him and his lips and his coffee taste and the rapid dissolution of all those years pretending she was over him.

Ethan devoured her mouth on a surge of longing so all-consuming his knees almost buckled. But he felt her give against him and he held on to her tight, holding them both up in the maelstrom that descended.

He was lost in a heady cloud of want that he hadn't experienced in a long time. Ama and the near disaster they'd avoided was forgotten, the Hunter Clinic was forgotten, Fair Go was forgotten, even Aaliyah was forgotten as an all-consuming surrender stormed his body.

Olivia had got under his skin and ploughed through his defences. Her mouth was as sweet as he remembered—sweeter—like a revelation, like a homecoming. Her breathing was heavy—like a rough panting in his head. And when his tongue entered her mouth she made a soft whimpering noise at the back of her throat that took him way back to the beginning, to when she hadn't been able to keep her hands off him.

Back to when he could have had her any time, anywhere, anyhow.

And nothing else had mattered.

He didn't stop to think about consequences or regrets or common sense. The need to have her, to reacquaint himself with *every* delectable inch of her, swamped *every* cell in a dire imperative to mate and he followed where it led, hopeless to resist.

He moved according to the dictates of his body. He kissed and he touched and he felt, his senses filling with her, intoxicating him with desire, his head humming with the need to be skin on skin, to feel her under him, to move deep inside her.

Before he knew it her scrub top was up and off and his hands were full of the soft mounds of her breasts, her nipples hard and ready in his palms. Then he was moving his hands down, pushing under the waistband of her scrubs, cupping her naked bottom, pushing them down her hips and off, conscious on some level that she was kicking out of them.

And then she was naked and he needed just to look at her, to remember every naked inch of her. To take her in and familiarise himself with the pure visual delight of her.

She didn't protest as he picked her up, his mouth still joined to hers, their tongues duelling and clashing, their mouths trying to suck up as much of the other as they could.

He laid her on the bed and she looked just as he remembered: long and lean and utterly lovely. Lust had honed his night vision and he could see her nipples were pale and puckered tight. Her hair had escaped its messy up-do and was now spread out around her head like a cloud. Her half-closed eyes and pouty full lips were so damn sexy he almost lost it right then and there.

Olivia's head spun. She was so alive with the touch and taste of him she was practically levitating off the bed.

'Ethan…' she half sighed, half moaned, and held her arms out to him.

Ethan didn't need any further encouragement. He was suddenly awake, bursting with life and passion, and Olivia was his Princess Charming.

She'd kissed him and woken him from a long sleep. A wellspring of desire he'd thought long dead was grabbing fiery possession of his groin and tugging hard.

He was out of his clothes in seconds, his erection, hard and urgent, springing gratefully free of the confines of his trousers, and as he joined her on the bed, his mouth lowering to rejoin hers again, her hand slipped along the length of him.

'Oh…' He groaned into her mouth as she gripped his girth just the way he liked it—good and firm.

Olivia revelled in the harsh scratch of his whiskers and in his guttural groan. And the way he filled her palm… *Dear Lord.* He'd always been big and solid, but feeling him again was like coming home, and when she stroked him she remembered just the way he liked it—as if it had been imprinted into her memory banks forever.

But he remembered about her as well, and she arched her back, gasping into his mouth as one hand slid to a breast and the other found its way to the slick folds at the juncture of her legs, stroking her just right too. Just the way she liked it—good and firm.

Olivia's head buzzed with the overload of sensations. But it wasn't enough. She wanted him inside her. Pounding hard and deep. Panting in her ear. Wanted to listen to him coming undone.

To come undone with him.

'Now, Ethan,' she said. *'Now.'*

Ethan heard and understood her demand for what it was—a call of the wild. The irrevocable need to mate, to be one. And maybe he should have been strong enough to resist it, to make this long and slow, to tease and taunt, to bring her to orgasm first before succumbing to his own overriding desire to be part of her.

But all the wasted years battered against him and he didn't want to waste another second.

'Ethan!' she called again.

He knew a sexual demand when he heard it, and he knew she needed him to be inside her as much as he needed to be there too.

He didn't think about anything other than her as she wrapped her legs around his waist, inhaling the smell of his soap on the skin of her neck as he buried his face there and thrust into her, sliding home, deep and sure, on a groan that seemed to echo up from the mists of time.

He didn't think about their history. He didn't think about Ama or the emergency trache he'd had to perform. He didn't think about his injuries.

He didn't think about Aaliyah.

He didn't even think about a condom.

He just let the sound of her gasp fill his head and the dig of her nails ground him to the bed and the frantic rhythm of their bodies take him away.

This was Olivia, and it was as if they'd never been apart.

'Yes,' she said. 'Oh, God…please, yes…don't stop…'

Ethan had no intention of stopping. He just held her tight and thrust over and over, her gasps pushing him higher and higher, urging him on, his heart-rate ratcheting up with each erotic slide of flesh into flesh.

Hard, hot, delicious tension coiled in his shoulders, buttocks and the backs of his thighs. Fire raged out of control in his loins and spread to his belly. It built to an inferno until every muscle burned and shook from the unbearable tautness.

'Let go, Ethan,' she whispered. 'Let go.'

And he did. In a shocking jolt everything snapped and he fell headlong into ecstasy, slipping his hand between them into all her slick heat, finding just the right spot and stroking her there as his world came apart, aware of her muscles clamping down tight around him and the sharp keening of her cry as she joined him.

And he kept rocking and thrusting, riding it out, keeping it going, until the last shudder had undulated through him and the last cry had been wrung from her mouth.

Until they were both spent and lying on their backs, gasping for breath and reaching for sanity, fighting and losing the battle to keep heavy lids open.

# CHAPTER NINE

OLIVIA DIDN'T KNOW where she was when she first woke. It was dark and everything was unfamiliar. She was used to that, travelling so much, but this felt different.

It took several more seconds for the warm pillow beneath her head to register as human. Warm, male, human.

*Holy crap!*

She sat up as everything came crashing back. Ethan's apartment. Il Conte's spaghetti. A warm shower. A bronze figurine. Urgent, need-you-now sex.

Really great, need-you-now sex.

Ethan stirred, shifted, mumbled something and rolled on his side but didn't wake. He'd always been a heavy sleeper—something that apparently the military hadn't cured him of. But given how exhausted they'd both been it wasn't surprising.

But *she* was wide-awake. Panic skittered along her veins and edged up her heart-rate.

Crap! She'd slept with Ethan-freaking-Hunter. The one man on this earth she'd vowed she'd never, ever sleep with again! *Good going, Olivia. Really smart move. Nothing like taking a giant leap backwards in your evolution as a human being. Why not just give the man your heart on a platter and a great big knife to stab right through the centre of it?*

*Did you learn nothing?*

But then another thought came crashing through her self-loathing. *Ama.*

*Oh, hell!* She leapt from the bed, her heart-rate ratcheting up another notch—what was the time? She had to get back to the hospital.

Olivia could barely think straight as she dashed around, trying to find her scrubs and get dressed in the dark, trying and failing to leave the bedroom without a backward glance and annoyed at herself when the broad sweep of a naked shoulder made the muscles deep inside her belly twist—in a good way.

A really good way.

*Damn it!*

She forced herself out into the still lit hallway and the even brighter open-plan lounge/kitchen. She found her shoes near the lounge and shoved her feet in. Grabbed her coat discarded on a kitchen stool and shoved her arms in. Then she shoved fingers through her hair and hoped to hell it didn't look as if she'd just rolled out of bed with a man who was a very bad bet.

She snagged her bag as she hurried past the counter heading for the door, digging around in it for her phone, finding it as she reached the knob, and yanked the door open, clicking it shut behind her as she scrolled through, looking for any missed calls or messages.

*None.*

Her shoulders sagged in relief as she hit the stairs. But it wasn't enough—she needed to know more. Olivia speed-dialled the ICU as she scurried down the stairs. A nurse answered as her foot hit the bottom step and by the time she was out of the apartment and striding towards the hospital she'd ascertained that Ama was stable, sedated and doing well.

'I'll be there in five minutes,' Olivia informed the nurse, then hit the end button.

Only then did she notice other things. Like her frantic breath misting into the air, the cold slapping into her face as she all but burst into a jog on the footpath, the sting in her thighs as needles of frosty air penetrated the cotton of her scrubs.

Olivia pulled the collar up on her duffle coat and tightened the belt, hunching into its thick layers for added warmth. *It was freezing.* She'd forgotten how cold London was in November.

It had been warm in Africa.

*It had been even warmer in Ethan's bed.*

What *had* she been thinking? *The man feeds her spaghetti and keeps a dumb memento from their time together and she just opens her legs for him?*

The slight ache there mocked her for her stupidity, as did the dampness slicking her inner thighs. They hadn't even used a damn condom. Two *doctors* who should *know* better and they hadn't even stopped to be responsible!

She hadn't thought. Or cared. She'd just needed him inside her.

Her brisk footfalls were loud on the deserted pavement and each one formed the rhythm to her self-loathing.

*Stupid. Stupid. Stupid.*

*Idiot. Idiot. Idiot.*

*Fool. Fool. Fool.*

Olivia was grateful when she rounded the corner and the lights of the hospital were just there—close enough to reach out and touch. Like a beacon of hope, saving her from a bitchy internal dialogue and a series of thoughts that could only get more ugly.

She couldn't worry about any of the Ethan stuff right now.

They *were* going to need to talk, but for tonight—until Ama was out of the woods—she didn't want to think about anything else. She certainly didn't want to have a *conversation* with him when their sex was still on her skin and his kisses still imprinted on her mouth.

And, if she knew Ethan at all, he wouldn't be cherishing the idea of talking either. Hell, they'd spent months together a decade ago and he clearly hadn't spoken to her at all—not about anything of import. About what was going on with him, about his pain and anger. Clamming up and being all brooding and silent seemed to be his speciality.

And, for once, Olivia was glad of it.

Ethan woke with a start. Aaliyah's laughter was a faint echo in his head, teasing him somewhere in the distance, fluttering elusively just out of his reach, like a ribbon in the breeze.

But in his mind's eyes he tried anyway, his hand extending, grabbing nothing but air.

*Same as always.*

*Aaliyah. I'm so sorry, Aaliyah.*

Gloomy daylight bled in around the heavy curtains at his window, matching his mood to perfection. The low hum of London traffic was a fitting background to the mumbled recriminations of his thoughts.

He rolled his head to the side, where his arm was flung out on the mattress. The empty space was cold: no hint of bodily warmth, no dent in the pillow beside him to indicate anyone had been there.

Same as always. *But not.*

Olivia was long gone and he was…*relieved*.

He sat up in bed on a groan, his nudity mocking him. The smell of Olivia, of their joining, infused his senses, refusing to let it be just another bad dream. He ploughed his fingers into the cropped hair covering his bowed head.

'Aaliyah,' he whispered.

*Hell.* He'd promised her he'd love her only. *I'm so sorry, my love.*

And now he'd betrayed two women. Aaliyah *and* Olivia.

Olivia, who deserved better than some half-man, physically *and* emotionally crippled.

But, damn it! She'd got under his skin. Like she had last time. Sneaked in under his defences. And for a little while last night he'd felt alive again. He'd been relying on his work to do that for him this past six months. And it had been working.

But last night…

'Damn it!'

Ethan swung his legs over the bed. Work had been *more* than fulfilling for him. He'd felt accomplished. He'd felt as if he was making a difference—especially when he'd thought his days of making a difference were over.

When he'd been medically discharged from the military he'd doubted he would ever be fulfilled again. But Leo had given him a way and Ethan had been proud of the Hunter Clinic's humanitarian programme, developed and nurtured under his leadership.

And after Aaliyah that was all he'd needed. He was done with everything else. Emotions, relationships. And resigned to it.

And then along came Olivia.

And he'd screwed it up a second time. Done something completely unforgivable. Not only betraying the memory of the woman he'd been going to marry but by reaching for Olivia again, whom he'd promised to leave alone.

*Goddamn it!*

Ethan rose from the bed, a slow burn of anger replacing his gloom and disappointment. How could he have done it? Where was his iron-clad self-control? Where was his single-minded focus? Where was *his word*, damn it?

He'd promised Aaliyah he'd love her only.

Then he'd promised her he'd come back for her. And just last week he'd promised Olivia he'd keep his hands off.

All broken.

It seemed he was destined in this life to let everyone down, to destroy all that he held dear. People he loved got hurt, went away. His mother had died and he'd never stopped missing her, even when the truth about her had come to light. And Aaliyah. So passionate and dedicated. Gone too.

But Olivia, who'd had enough heartache of her own, was still alive, and after nearly destroying her once he *wouldn't* do that again. He operated best alone, where he couldn't hurt anyone.

He stalked into the bathroom, with a slow simmer of anger in his belly and a skinful of self-loathing for company. He flicked the cold tap on and stepped straight under the spray, hoping to hose them off enough to be able to function today.

Hoping he could hose Olivia away as easily.

Olivia was at Ama's bedside when Ethan arrived half an hour later. Ril and Dali had ducked out to get some breakfast. She looked up as he swept into the isolation room. He was in a dark suit with a russet tie and if anything he looked more haggard than ever. The lines she'd first noted around his eyes at their reunion were back with a vengeance and his stubble was now almost a soft beard.

But the flecks in his eyes flared briefly as his gaze roved over her—checking her for signs of damage, she assumed—and her heart gave a funny lurch in her chest.

And then she remembered how stupid she'd been. How those golden flecks had made her lose her head. *And her clothes.*

And how her focus had to be Ama.

Ethan watched her expression cool and followed her lead. 'Olivia.' He nodded.

Olivia felt absurdly close to tears at the formality in his voice and the stiffness of his expression. *What the...?* Clearly some recalcitrant part of her had been hoping that he'd tear down all her well-reasoned objections and whisk her up in his arms. But, like her, he'd obviously decided to focus on Ama and keep things strictly professional between them.

And that was a *good* thing.

'Ethan.' She nodded too, then turned back to Ama.

Ethan hadn't been sure what he was going to say or how he was going to act this morning but her coolness helped him decide. Mutual professional respect was the only way forward. They had to see each other and they had to work together, both now and in the future. And to do that they had to forget what had come before. Forget their baggage. Maintain a strictly collegial relationship.

And keep the hell away from each other in between times.

Hadn't they already agreed to that anyway?

*And failed.*

Ethan pushed it all away, slipping into a skin he knew well—*Mr Hunter.* 'How is she this morning?' he asked.

They had a ten-minute conversation about Ama's progress and the plan for the next few days, which involved removing the tracheostomy and getting her out of ICU. Ril and Dali returned then, and Ethan and Olivia had a long talk with them about the previous night and what the next days and the next steps were for Ama.

Ril was worried about her daughter still, but encouraged by her progress, and Olivia assured her again that she would be with them all until Ama was well enough to go home and she would be the one taking them back to Africa.

Ril smiled as Dali translated, patting and rubbing Olivia's arm, nodding and speaking words of gratitude in her own tongue as tears shone in her eyes. Olivia was extraordinarily moved by Ril's faith.

When Ril was satisfied she returned to the chair by her daughter's bed and Ethan turned to Olivia and said, 'They want us to sit in on the ICU round—you want to join me?'

Olivia nodded. She did want to be able to co-ordinate Ama's care with the ICU doctors.

'It's starting now. Shall we?' he said, and indicated for her to precede him out of the room.

Olivia told Dali where they were going and then walked ahead of Ethan, conscious of his gaze on her back. Conscious that only a handful of hours ago she'd been in his bed. Conscious that, under her coat, she was wearing the same clothes he'd stripped her out off. That his smell clung to her skin. That the evidence of her arousal and their unprotected sex had mingled to feel all hot and slick between her legs.

'Whereabouts?' she asked, her head slightly turned.

Ethan fell into step beside her. 'End of the corridor, turn right, third door on the left.'

She didn't acknowledge him, just followed along silently beside him, and he took a breath and broached the subject of the elephant stomping along beside them.

'About last night…' he said.

'No.' Olivia shook her head vigorously, not breaking stride as her heart did a crazy leap in her chest. She'd been sure he'd be in ostrich mode. 'Let's not do this, okay?'

Ethan tried to keep it casual as they walked down the very public corridor. He wanted to get this thing between them on to an even keel as fast as possible, and the only way to do that was to clear the air about what had happened at his place last night.

They couldn't just pretend it hadn't happened. That was a sure-fire way to breed resentment.

'We *do* need to talk about it, Olivia. Hell,' he said lowering his voice, 'I didn't even use a condom.'

That particular little gem had come to him in the shower.

The fact that it hadn't even crossed his mind at the appropriate time had been shocking. He wished it had—not least of all because he didn't have a condom anywhere in his apartment and that would definitely have brought them both to their senses. There'd certainly be no need for this awkward morning-after conversation, walking down a busy corridor in a *children's hospital*, whispering about unprotected sex as if they were teenagers!

'You think I don't know that?' Olivia demanded. 'I'm not wearing any underwear. Trust me, I know. And I know we need to talk about this, and we will,' she said. 'Just *not now*. Not while Ama's still in ICU, okay?'

Ethan nodded, clamping down hard on the leap in his pulse and the hitch in his breath at the thought of her going commando. Things stirred and he battered them down with all the authority of a dictator crushing a revolt.

He cleared his throat. 'Okay, sure,' he agreed.

'Thank you,' she said.

And they both continued in silence.

That was pretty much the pattern for the next few days. Quick, professional meetings involving stilted conversations about Ama and her progress. Nothing personal, just medical.

Day two post-op Ama's tracheostomy was removed and she was moved to HDU. They had none of the opiate problems that had been the catalyst for her post-op bleed and Ama, although quiet and exhausted from her unexpected complications, improved every day.

Two days later she was back on the ward and Olivia was finally starting to feel that they had turned a corner. Ama wasn't back to her full cheeky, happy self, but she was showing interest in the world around her again and even asked for the television to be put on.

Olivia thought that was real progress, and for the first time since the operation actually allowed herself to think about other things.

Naturally her thoughts turned to Ethan.

Ethan, on the other hand, whilst exceedingly pleased with Ama's progress too, was increasingly crotchety and frustrated.

He hadn't been able to sleep since Olivia had slept in his bed. At first he'd thought it was just her scent keeping him up, but he'd changed the sheets to no avail.

He lay awake for hours, his brain circling around what he'd done, his gut heavy, and when he slept it was with strange dreams of Aaliyah and Olivia. He was chasing them both as they ran from him, teasing him with their laughter, only to catch one and watch as her face blended into the other. Changing back and forth until he didn't know whether he was holding Aaliyah or Olivia.

It took him two sleepless nights to realise that

the feeling of a lead weight in his belly was his guilt flaring to life again. This bed had belonged to Aaliyah, even though she'd never slept in it. She'd come to him in his dreams here, and as much as they'd tortured him with their heart-breaking clarity they'd also kept him close to her.

He'd used to welcome the night and sleep, when he could be with her again.

But now Olivia was in the bed too. In his head. And the guilt was eating him up.

After that realisation the dreams changed. They became bloody and disturbing. They became nightmares. Slices of that awful day when all hell had broken loose magnified tenfold in his head.

The heat and the smoke. The noise of bombs and gunfire. The blood. The carnage.

Aaliyah's, *'Go, Ethan, I'll be fine,'* played like a broken record, waking him in a cold sweat.

Driving him out of the bed. *Their* bed. But not any more. Because Olivia was in it too. In his head again.

The empty bed mocked him. He was alive and getting naked with Olivia when Aaliyah was dead. Dead because he hadn't got back to her in time.

A few weeks ago he would have poured himself a drink or twelve. But something had changed—he didn't seem to crave it as he had. As his father had.

Ethan had worried that there was some genetic component and he would turn out like his old man, become the type of person he'd despised in his father.

It was a relief to realise he didn't *need* it.

He headed for his home gym instead and pounded it out on the leg press and treadmill. Filling his head with Aaliyah, trying not to think about Olivia. Trying to exercise—exorcise—his guilt into oblivion. Trying to exhaust himself.

He needed to sleep.

A tired surgeon made mistakes!

On the morning of day five Olivia was going slightly stir-crazy from spending all day cooped up in the hospital. She hadn't had any form of exercise in weeks now and she was beginning to feel it. As a jogger, she usually pounded the pavements wherever she was, but going out in a freezing London morning was not something she welcomed.

Instead she decided to take up Leo on his offer of using the Hunter Clinic pool in the basement next to the gym. It was heated, and she could slip in there early, while no one was around, do some laps and be dressed and at the hospital by eight.

She needed to do *something*. Dali had texted her to say that Ama wanted to see her new face. They'd all seen it and were very happy with how it looked—Ril had even cried—but Ama hadn't been interested. Olivia had been concerned about her reaction but Ethan had put it down to her extended recovery time and assured her it was fine, that Ama would get to it in her own time. That she needed to be ready.

And she was ready today.

Olivia was both nervous and excited, with butterflies dancing in her stomach whenever she thought about how Ama might react. She hoped she would be pleased. She hoped the old cheeky Ama would be back.

But in the interim she had to do something to

rid herself of her nervous energy and, lucky for her, she always packed a swimsuit wherever she went!

Ethan increased the speed on the treadmill, trying to outrun the thoughts pounding through his head. He was using the clinic gym because his whole apartment, not just his bed, seemed to remind him of Olivia now. After being away from it for a decade and coming back to it again with Aaliyah's death still so fresh, it, along with his head space, had felt exclusively hers.

The place they would have lived. The kitchen they would have cooked in. The couch they would have snuggled on.

The bed they would have slept in.

But now Olivia was there too.

Sure, she'd been there before. Had spent a lot of time at his place. But that had been a long time ago—in a different lifetime practically. When he'd been spoiled and angry and unworthy of her love. Of anyone's love.

When he'd thought he'd been as injured as he could possibly be. *Man—had he been mistaken!*

Because a lot had happened since then. Aaliyah. His injuries. And now Olivia.

Who was everywhere in his apartment.

He'd had to get out.

Olivia heard a machine's noise and some grunting as she headed to the pool/gym area and hesitated for a second. She'd thought this early she'd be here by herself. But all she wanted to do was swim. A little bit of splashing surely wouldn't disturb anyone doing a workout. Especially not if they were making that much noise.

And maybe it was Leo. She needed to give him an Ama update anyway.

But as she walked closer she realised it wasn't Leo. It was Ethan. He wasn't wearing a shirt, exposing his broad back and shoulders completely to her view. A back and shoulders she'd know anywhere. The same back and shoulders she'd clung to the other night as he'd pounded into her like a man possessed.

Sweat beaded on his nape and in the furrow of his spine as his traps, rhomboids and lats bunched and relaxed with each yank on the rowing machine handle. He was gliding frantically back and forth on the seat as if he was rowing for gold—or trying to outrun his demons.

Olivia almost turned and walked away and left him to his punishing exercise. There was no way he could have heard her above the noise of the machine and his own significant exertion. But they still hadn't talked, and she figured now Ama was better and they were alone it was as good a time as any.

She took a breath and continued towards him, leaning her butt against a nearby bench press apparatus.

Ethan started as the woman he'd been trying to row out of his head appeared beside him in a white fluffy robe tied loosely at the waist.

He almost groaned out loud. Did she *have* to be everywhere?

He turned back to concentrate on his workout, zoning her out of his peripheral vision as he regained his rhythm and rowed harder.

Olivia watched him ignoring her for a few moments, his eyes locked on the screen in front of him, where his programmed workout was ticking down. Her gaze dropped to his chest. She hadn't meant it to—it just did. The light smattering of hair across his pecs and bisecting his belly was so familiar to her, yet she didn't recall being conscious of it the other night.

Nothing but his mouth on hers and his hardness inside her had registered.

Annoyed at the direction of her thoughts, she folded her arms and asked in a raised voice, 'So, are there any sexually transmitted diseases I should know about?'

# CHAPTER TEN

OLIVIA WAS SORRY that she got no discernible reaction from Ethan save for a tightening of his jaw. He just continued to pull on the handle of the rower and glide back and forth with powerful precision.

She wasn't actually worried about it. She was on the pill and Ethan, for all he could have been with his looks and his money, had never been a man whore. Or casual with contraception. They'd had a *lot* of sex and never *not* used a condom, despite her already being protected against pregnancy.

But it *had* been ten years, and in lots of ways the man before her was more of a stranger now than he'd ever been.

And weren't men in uniform supposed to have women throwing themselves in their paths?

Her gaze dropped to the bunching of muscles

in his arms as they bent and straightened, bent and straightened. Ethan must have been a sight to behold in combat gear. All tall and broad, his tight butt emphasised by his long-legged stride. What girl could have resisted that when combined with his charming smile and his penchant for going all shaggy with his stubble?

She could imagine him right at home in some rocky barren landscape in the middle of nowhere, doing what he did best—saving lives.

A minute later the machine beeped and Ethan, his thighs screaming, eased back on the pace, gliding up and down the rower more sedately now as he allowed his muscles and his temper time to cool down.

Olivia had been in his head and his dreams for the past five nights and now she was here, busting his balls. He refused to look at her, to answer her, until he was totally chilled.

When the cool-down period ended he finally pushed the seat back into the starting position, took his feet out of the foot plates and grounded them on the floor. He picked up his towel from beside the machine and dried off his head, nape and chest, then looped it around his neck and hung onto the tails.

'You're joking, right?' he said as he finally turned his head to look at her.

His eyes had gone from dull to downright chilly and Olivia suppressed a shiver. He seemed even further away than ever. 'I don't know you any more, Ethan.'

Ethan returned her gaze unflinchingly. 'You know me.'

God, if anyone knew him it was her. Not even Aaliyah had known him so warts and all. She'd only seen the good side of him, working side by side with him in a remote civilian hospital, swept up in the life and death of it all.

Easy to be heroic.

It was Olivia who had seen all the ugly stuff too.

Olivia looked away from the intensity of his eyes, her gaze dropping to the floor. She didn't want to think about the truth of his words. She shrugged. 'Maybe you had a girl in every port?'

Ethan's hands gripped the towel harder. There'd been very few women since Olivia and no one serious. Not until he'd totally lost his heart to Aaliyah anyway. 'I wasn't in the freaking navy, Olivia.'

Olivia toed the thin floor-covering. 'So you're clean?'

Ethan nodded. 'Yes. And I take it you are also—and still on the pill?'

It was Olivia's turn to nod. 'Good,' she said, prising her eyes off the ground. 'I guess we've had our talk, then.'

But they didn't get all the way to his face. Her gaze snagged on the bulk of an exposed quad. A quad deeply furrowed by the criss-cross of pink scar tissue, each deep fissure naked of the dark blond hair covering the rest of his thigh.

'Oh, God, Ethan…' she gasped, looking up at him and then back down at his legs, seeking the other exposed quad too, shocked at the state of them. 'Bloody hell…'

Ethan quickly whipped the towel off his neck and threw it across his lap. 'It's nothing,' he dismissed, cursing himself for not thinking. His gym shorts came to just below his knee—more than adequate cover—but he hadn't counted on the hem riding up to expose his injuries.

Or for her to be here.

The only person who had ever seen his scars apart from the myriad doctors and nurses who had treated him in hospital was Lizzie, who'd had the unenviable job of dressing his stubborn wounds as his home care nurse.

Olivia felt hot tears spike at her eyes. This was not *nothing*! No wonder his legs had almost given out on him that first time they'd seen each other again. She felt awful. They'd both been naked together the other night and she'd been more interested in having him inside her than worrying about his wounds or checking out his body.

Before she knew what she was doing she'd dropped to her knees beside him, pushing the towel aside. 'Ethan,' she whispered, looking up at him and then looking back down, one tentative finger following a deep ridge from one side of his thigh to the other.

She remembered that he'd said gunfire had caused his injuries and looking at them objectively, as a doctor, she knew it to be true. She'd seen too many bullet wounds in Africa.

*Dear God, the pain he must have gone through.*

And then without conscious thought she was lowering her mouth to where her finger had been. Kissing him better. Knowing that it was too little too late. Hating that he'd been so terribly wounded. That she'd judged him so harshly.

Ethan looked at her downcast head. The brush of her lips against the numb edges of his wounds and the caress of her honey-brown hair was strangely erotic.

*He wasn't strong enough for this.*

He'd just spent an hour trying to exorcise the memory of her. Trying to recapture the essence of Aaliyah. Her stoic, haunted beauty. Her steady, calming presence.

'Olivia…' he murmured, shutting his eyes, touched by her empathy, aroused by the visual of her bent head over his legs, the feel of her mouth hot against his thigh. Hating that something so obviously emotional, that gouged at his gut, also yanked at his groin. How could something so innocent be so sexual?

She had to stop. Or he was going to do something he regretted. The loathing he felt for himself cranked up another notch.

'Olivia!'

Olivia raised her head and looked at him as she sat back on her haunches. He looked torn, and the flecks in his eyes were glowing again, like the flash of fire in her opal ring. 'I hate that this happened to you,' she said. 'I just want to be able to…take it all away. To go back…'

Go back to the beginning. To stay and fight for him rather than storming out in a fit of pique. Even if he had deserved it. Maybe he wouldn't have joined up. Maybe she could have helped mend the rift between him and Leo.

Ethan shook his head. 'You can't,' he said, fighting against the compassion he saw in her eyes.

'How did this happen?' she whispered.

Ethan shook his head. His heart was clinging desperately to Aaliyah, to the promises he'd made her, but other parts of him wanted to scoop Olivia up, press her into the hard floor of the gym and fill the entire cavernous room with her cries.

To forget about how it had happened.

But he'd hurt her once before and he wasn't going to screw up his life—or her life—again with the mess that was in his head. There'd been enough loss in his life and he wasn't going to spread any collateral damage.

He wasn't a good bet. He knew that.

*But she needed to know that.*

He didn't want her to see him like this—as some man crippled by what had happened to him. As an object of sympathy. He didn't want her sympathy. She needed to stop thinking of him as some wounded man and remember how he'd crushed her heart into the dust.

Pulling himself together, looking down at the ugly ridges that marred his skin, he was glad now though that she *had* seen them.

They were his constant reminder that he'd let Aaliyah down. That he didn't deserve a woman's love.

A tsunami of anger rolled inside him. She wanted to know how it had happened? *Fine.*

'There was this woman,' he said, glancing at her. 'Another doctor. Aaliyah. Aaliyah Hassan.'

Olivia swallowed at the way he said her name. There was a softness there—an affection. He'd sure as hell never said *her* name that way.

'I was working with her in a remote hospital in the south,' Ethan said. He paused and took a swig of water from the bottle on the ground beside the rower. 'They got a lot of civilian and military wounded through there,' he said, staring into the bottle. 'I was kind of…seconded there with some other medical personnel for quite some time. She was…amazing.'

Olivia didn't need him to say it. The truth of it was in the melting of his eyes and the way her stomach fell. 'You loved her.'

Ethan looked at Olivia. 'Yes. We were engaged to be married.'

Olivia was surprised how much it hurt and immediately castigated herself. Had she thought a decade later he'd be pining away for *her* somewhere, regretting his actions?

They'd both got on with their lives.

'What happened?'

'The area where the hospital was situated came under attack one day. We had to evacuate. It was…carnage.' Ethan shuddered at the memory. 'Aaliyah and I and a team from the base worked for hours on the evac, with shells landing all round us. It was almost done—we just had two criticals and another six patients to get to safety—and I told Aaliyah to go with them, that I'd wait behind. But they'd been her patients and she didn't want to leave them. She told me to go. There were some of my guys there for her protection, so I left.'

Olivia shut her eyes. She knew how this was going to end even before he finished—even before she looked down to see him kneading the scarred flesh of his thighs as if he was trying to pull it off his bones.

'I told her I'd be back for her in thirty minutes.' He looked up from his legs at her. 'They only had to wait another thirty minutes.'

Olivia nodded as she opened her eyes. 'You didn't get back in time?'

Ethan raked a hand through his sweaty hair. 'I did. We did. Two ambulances got back within thirty minutes. I was pushing one of the gurneys across to the entrance. Then this gunfire came out of nowhere, slamming into my legs, and I was falling to the ground. And then a shell slammed into the building and it just blew…it was…*flattened*. And I don't remember anything after that…not until I woke up in a field hospital.'

Olivia didn't need him to say the words. It was obvious that his fiancée had died in the building. 'And you feel guilty?'

He glared at her. 'You think I shouldn't?' He snorted.

Olivia knew a lot about this kind of guilt. *Survivor guilt.* 'You think you should have been in that building instead of her?'

'Yes. I wanted her out. I'd been trying to get her to evac with the others all day.'

'So…you'd be dead instead of her?'

'Yes,' he snapped.

Olivia tried not to flinch at his answer. She for one was pleased he hadn't been in the hospital when it had been flattened.

Ethan sighed. 'I don't know,' he said. 'Maybe things would have been different, would have gone down differently.'

Olivia nodded, knowing intimately how that

question had haunted her. 'Do you think me being with my parents that day would have made a difference?'

Ethan felt the question slice like a stiletto between his ribs. The thought of Olivia burning to death with her parents was too horrific to contemplate. 'That's not the same thing, Olivia.'

Olivia cocked an eyebrow at him. They both knew it was *exactly* the same thing. 'Do you think I should feel guilty about that?'

Ethan looked at the floor. 'Of course not.' He looked up at her. 'Do you?'

She shrugged. 'I did. For a long time.'

'And how did you get past it?' In the beginning his guilt had been paralysing. And even now, particularly since Olivia, it was too much for Ethan to bear.

'I realised I wasn't living.' Olivia drew in a shaky breath. It had taken her a long time to come to terms with that. 'And my parents wouldn't have wanted that any more than they'd have wanted me there with them in the vehicle that day.'

Ethan stared at the woman in front of him.

She'd been through a harrowing time a few years back. Had made the same kind of choice that he'd had to make. But she'd grown up in a stable, warm, loving environment and had always been well-adjusted.

He hadn't. He didn't have those kind of emotional building blocks. For all that he'd loved his mother, the truth was that she'd been a vain socialite who had rarely been at home and his father had been first a bombastic, domineering taskmaster who'd thrived on the rivalry he'd whipped up between his sons, then later a morose drunk.

Olivia waited for him to say something but his dull brown eyes seemed lost somewhere in the past. 'Do you think Aaliyah would blame you?' she pushed. 'Would want you to be blaming yourself?'

Ethan looked down at his legs, at the scars that reminded him every day of Aaliyah. Of how he'd let her down. *Of how he'd failed.*

He stood abruptly, the towel slipping off his shoulders. 'Don't say her name,' he said.

He couldn't bear to hear Aaliyah's name coming from Olivia's mouth. They were so mixed up in his head he couldn't deal with another variation.

Olivia blinked at the vehemence in his voice, striking right into her heart. She pushed out of her leaning position, standing up straight. 'Ethan?'

'What do you want?' he demanded, glaring down at her.

'To help you. I understand what you're going through.'

Yes, keeping out of his way would be wiser, but she couldn't walk away from him right now.

Not when he looked so gutted.

Ethan's lips curled. 'You don't understand,' he said contemptuously, aware he wasn't acting or sounding rational but unable to stop himself. She was looking at him with those eyes, all warm, gooey and compassionate, as if he deserved her empathy, and it made him even more incensed.

*Because he didn't.*

'Whatever it is you think I deserve, I don't,' he said. 'I loved her and I left her to *die*. Hell, Olivia, I *used* you to make my brother jealous. You once said that my relationship with Leo was toxic, but you know what? I think maybe it's just me that's toxic. Me that destroys everything good in my life. Maybe I'm just my father's son? On the path to self-destruction. I'm damaged goods, sweetheart.'

Olivia couldn't bear the raw pain in his voice but she knew Ethan needed to get this stuff off his chest. 'Were,' she said.

'No, don't do that, Olivia.' He shook his head vehemently. 'I know that look. Even when I was destroying you ten years ago, when you realised what I'd done, you looked at me with those dis-believing eyes. Like I *really* wasn't a bad per-son. Next you'll be dropping by to check on me and cooking me dinner. Don't build castles in the air over me. *I don't deserve it.* What I did to you, what I did to Aaliyah, they're imprinted in my brain. I can't just forget.'

Olivia blinked. Was that what she was doing? Was she building castles? Was she falling in love with him again? A man whose heart was buried in a foreign land with the woman he loved? A woman he couldn't forget?

She shut her eyes against the truth of it. *No. Please, no.*

It had been bad enough the first time around. Loving a man who hadn't loved her in return. Only this time she'd be competing with a ghost.

*She was a fool of the highest order.*

'What if I can make you forget?'

Olivia blinked as the words spilled into the tense space between them. She had no idea where they'd come from or even what she was offering. A relationship where he used her again? Or something more platonic, where she helped him work through his guilt?

And lost a bit of herself every day? Loving him with nothing in return?

*Oh, hell, she was a first class idiot.*

Ethan looked down at her, at the slice of cleavage he could see where the robe gaped. He had no doubt she could make him forget everything in a hundred different ways—she already had.

But it always came back.

And he'd just hate himself a little bit more. And so would she—eventually.

He lifted his left leg and placed his foot on the

apparatus beside her, the pink scars stretching as he leaned forward onto the leg. She looked down at them and then looked back up at him, her gaze killing him with her empathy.

'I have these to remind me,' he said bitterly.

Then he pushed off the machine, picked up his towel and water bottle from the floor and limped away without looking back.

Olivia swam up and down the twenty-five-metre pool non-stop for half an hour after that, her brain churning as she followed the black line.

*I love him. I love him. I love him.*

She was in love with Ethan Hunter. Again.

*Still.*

Had she ever really stopped? Sure, she'd despised him for a long time, and she'd buried herself in her work until it didn't hurt any more. But that wasn't the same as not *loving* him any more.

She hauled herself out of the pool, water sluicing off her, sitting on the edge in a puddle.

*Stupid.*

Stupid, crazy idiot.

Even more stupid now, given that Ethan was

in love with someone else. *A dead woman.* A woman whose death had trapped him in a cast-iron cage of guilt and penance where he didn't think he was deserving of love.

The mere thought both broke her heart and expanded the love in her chest even more.

*Prime*, numero uno *idiot*!

He'd made it clear that he wasn't going to let her in, that his heart belonged elsewhere, and she knew she couldn't go down that track with him again. She wasn't going to beat her head against the same brick wall she hadn't even realised she'd been beating her head against last time.

She had to have more self-respect than that, no matter how much Ethan's story tugged at her excessively sappy heartstrings!

He was right. No castles in the air for Ethan Hunter. Not this time.

Olivia's heavy thoughts dogged her all the way up to the clinic after she'd showered and changed. And she was still mired deep in the question of her sanity when she almost ran smack-bang into Lizzie, Leo's wife and the nurse in charge at the Hunter Clinic, as she stepped into the main section of the building from the basement stairs.

'Oh, sorry,' Olivia apologised, taking a moment or two to gather her thoughts.

Lizzie was in early. It was still barely seven-thirty. She'd crossed paths with the impressive head nurse a couple of times over the past few weeks and had been invited to their place next week for dinner.

'It's fine,' Lizzie dismissed with a quick smile. 'You look a little distracted.'

'What?' Olivia asked. 'Oh…no, sorry, just…' She shook her head. *Just what?* Inventing new and imaginative ways to murder your brother-in-law?

'Ah,' Lizzie said. 'I know that look. It's a man, yes?'

Olivia blinked. She was so stunned by the question she heard herself saying, 'Yes.'

'Come on,' Lizzie said. 'I have just the thing for that.'

Olivia glanced at her watch. She still had time, so she followed Lizzie to Leo's office. Lizzie headed for Leo's desk and Olivia hoped Lizzie wasn't going to offer her some medicinal whisky at seven-thirty in the morning.

Lizzie sat in Leo's chair, then reached down and to the side. Olivia heard a drawer opening and some riffling before Lizzie produced an intriguing flat box with beautifully embossed gold letters she couldn't quite make out.

Not that she needed to. Chocolate boxes looked pretty much the same the world over.

Lizzie opened the lid and inhaled appreciatively. She offered the box to Olivia who, despite not being a huge chocoholic, took one anyway.

'Leo always keeps a stash here for me. The baby has made this old sweet tooth even sweeter, and God alone knows I ate truckloads of the stuff when Leo and I were dancing around each other.'

Olivia unwrapped the golden foil and bit into the sweet treat. It melted on her tongue and fizzed seductively against her tastebuds. She shut her eyes as it rushed through her system. 'Mmm,' she said, opening her eyes. '*This* is good chocolate.'

Lizzie nodded enthusiastically as she picked a second out of the box. 'They're from the kingdom of Sirmontane. Marco—or I should say *Prince* Marco of Sirmontane, who Ethan patched up after being wounded in battle and who is engaged to Becca, our hand therapist—keeps me in constant supply. I've never been to a royal wedding before—I'm very excited.'

Olivia had tried not to flinch when Ethan's name was mentioned but it had been unexpected. She was pleased that Lizzie seemed too engrossed in reaching for a third chocolate to notice.

'Sirmontane is known for its excellence in chocolate,' Lizzie said, offering Olivia another, which she took without hesitation. 'Better than anything you'll get from Switzerland.'

Olivia nodded. It *was* exceptional chocolate. She'd heard about Prince Marco, and had met the lucky Becca once, but she hadn't known that Ethan had been his surgeon. Just the mention of his name took some of the sweetness out of the experience.

Lizzie nodded. 'The perfect antidote for what ails you, don't you think?'

Olivia nodded non-committally as she savoured the smooth rich flavour on her tongue. It really was quite spectacular, and had made her temporarily forget her man problems, but ever since Lizzie had said his name Ethan had become front and centre again.

Why did she have to love *him*?

Lizzie narrowed her gaze. 'I'm going to take a punt and guess that you're not thinking about the marvels of European chocolate?' she asked.

The sweetness coating her tongue turned to dust in her mouth and Olivia shrugged. 'No.'

'Are you thinking about Ethan?'

Olivia blinked. She liked Lizzie from what little she knew about her, but Olivia wasn't sure if she wanted to get into *this* with Lizzie, given the whole love triangle history she'd shared with Leo and Ethan.

'I do know, you know...about what happened ten years ago. Between you and Leo and Ethan.'

Olivia wasn't sure what she should say to that. Was Lizzie angry? Was she going to call her names or want pistols at dawn? 'Oh.'

'Leo thinks there might be a chance for you and Ethan this time around. A real chance. Do you love him?'

Okay. Now Olivia really didn't know what to

say. Lizzie sure didn't beat around the bush. 'I…
I…' What was the point in admitting it when it
was a futile thing to feel anyway?

'Do you know what happened to him on his
last tour?'

'Yes.' Olivia nodded, pleased to be able to answer one question at least. 'I read it in the paper
and he and I…we've talked about it since.'

Lizzie sat back in Leo's chair. 'He's been
through a lot. His injuries were horrific.'

'I know,' Olivia agreed. 'Not to mention
Aaliyah.'

Lizzie frowned. 'Aaliyah? Oh, you mean Dr
Hassan? The doctor that was killed when the
hospital was bombed? Yes. He hasn't really said
much about her, but I think he feels a degree of
guilt over that too. I think everything about that
day feeds into a significant case of PTSD.'

It was then Olivia realised that Lizzie didn't
know about Aaliyah. Didn't know that Ethan had
lost the woman he loved that day. Which probably meant that Leo didn't know either.

He hadn't told anybody.

*Except her.*

What the hell did that mean?

'Look,' Lizzie said, leaning a little closer and offering Olivia another chocolate. 'I know this is none of my business, but Ethan is kind of lost, and he needs someone to stick with him, and I think, by the way you flinched when I mentioned his name before, that you're probably the one to do it.'

Olivia shook her head. Lizzie might be well intentioned but there was a lot she clearly didn't know.

Lizzie raised her hand at Olivia's objection. 'I know these Hunter men. I know how they push you away. But I also know that they didn't exactly have warm and fuzzy upbringings and that they're hurting deep down inside—Ethan probably more so than Leo.'

Olivia admired how Lizzie was on Team Hunter. A wife should be. But... 'I don't think you know the full story,' she said tentatively.

'I know Ethan behaved reprehensibly,' Lizzie said. 'But if you love him, please, *please* don't give up on him.'

Olivia watched as Lizzie's hand fell to her

belly, to a baby that wasn't even on show yet. 'The Hunter men are worth the fight.'

Olivia felt absurdly like crying. If only it were that simple.

She knew how great it felt to be Ethan's woman. Even if he had been with her for all the wrong reasons he'd always been very attentive. Made her feel as if she *was* special. And she believed a lot of that had been genuine for him.

But there was another person now in their already complicated relationship. A woman he'd made it clear was his one and only love. How was she supposed to compete with Aaliyah?

Was she destined always to love a man who didn't love her back?

'Another?' Lizzie asked.

Olivia nodded. Why not? Chocolate was simpler than the problems that whizzed and clashed in her brain.

And it might be the closest she'd ever come to gratification again.

She found the biggest one and sank her teeth into it.

## CHAPTER ELEVEN

THREE DAYS LATER Ethan stood in the doorway of Ama's hospital room and watched as Ama admired herself—actually, *preened* was probably a better word—in front of a small hand-held mirror. She angled her head from side to side and brought the mirror closer for a moment or two, before taking it back to appreciate a wider frame.

She'd been looking at herself in the mirror practically non-stop since she'd first seen her new face a few days ago, and he never got tired of seeing her reaction. She still had the staples in her graft, and there was residual swelling around the operative area, but her face was now 'whole' and it was obvious Ama was thrilled with the result.

Yes, they had more work to do in the next couple of months, and the dressing over Ama's trachea from her healing stoma was a constant reminder that not everything had gone smoothly. But the aesthetic part of the reconstructive surgery had been an outstanding success.

Olivia was clearly ecstatic with the result. He watched her as she sat on the bed in front of Ama, and even though Ethan could only see her in profile he knew she was grinning broadly at Ama's mirror antics. He enjoyed the sight for long moments, because the minute she saw him it would all change.

She'd been cool towards him the past few days. Not that he could blame her. He'd pushed her away in his need to cling to Aaliyah and this was the result. But still, he hated to see the distance in her gaze, hated the walls between them even though he was responsible for them.

Even though he knew it was the best way forward.

As he watched, Olivia gave Ama the pen torch and he could see the girl's eyes shining from way across the other side of the room. Ethan remembered how Olivia had talked about having children one day. He thought about all the kids at the Lighthouse he'd seen her with too. She was a natural and, watching her with Ama, he knew she'd make a great mother.

Something stirred in his chest at the thought of what her babies might look like—stirred, tugged, kicked—but he quashed it. Whatever mini-Olivias looked like it was none of his damn concern.

Ama giggled and dragged his attention back to the room. She popped the pen torch into the side of her mouth that hadn't been operated on and, with her mouth closed, flicked it on. Ama watched as her cheek glowed red in the mirror and she laughed so hard Ethan thought she was going to fall off the bed. It was so infectious, so joyous, so innocent—as it should be—he couldn't help joining in.

He saw Olivia's back stiffen slightly as he entered the room but she turned and gave him a small smile, and even if her eyes were cool her demeanour was one hundred per cent professional as she stood politely.

Ethan sat on the bed where Olivia had been and there was some more playing with the torch, and Ama, who'd really come out of the shell she'd been in post-op, chatted as if she'd been mute all her life and had just found her voice. Dali was scrambling to keep up with her and Ethan laughed at her enthusiasm.

He glanced at Olivia, who was looking down at Ama with affection in her gaze. Was she thinking the same as he was? Would Ama have been this carefree—this animated, this happy—if she'd been married off at such a young age?

Was she thinking about the potential Ama had now?

Olivia had literally given this lucky little girl her life back.

'Well, I think you are way too well to be in hospital, Little Miss,' Ethan said, looking back at Ama. 'I think it's time you went and stayed with your host family until your next operation.'

Olivia watched Ril and Ama's face as Dali translated. They were so rapturously happy she could feel tears scalding the backs of her eyes. Fair Go had sourced an African family to host Ril and Ama in between surgeries, and she knew how much they were both looking forward to some familiarity.

There was a flurry of excitement in the room and it was hard for Olivia not to get caught up in it. She'd been keeping herself in check around Ethan, but when he smiled at her with a *how-great-is-this?* look in his eyes she found herself smiling back.

It *was* great. Apart from a hiccup or two, Ama's surgery had been successful and that was something to celebrate. There was no reason to be churlish because their personal baggage sat like a loaded luggage carousel between them.

But when he cocked his head to indicate he wanted to talk to her outside she felt the barriers going up. The man was rocking a pair of scrubs again and she really wasn't strong enough for this.

Now Ama was being discharged there was no need to see Ethan on a regular basis until Ama came back in for her next scheduled op. And once Ama was back in Africa Olivia would be gone also. Sure, she'd be coming back and forth to London on charity business, and she'd also be in phone and email contact with him, but that would be so much easier than this.

Having to face him so soon after their talk in the gym, after realising she still loved him, was too hard. She could accept that she loved him, and that he'd never return that love, but not if he was parading around in her deepest secret fantasy garb, taunting her with what would never be hers.

Olivia took steadying breaths as she stepped into the corridor with him, hoping this wasn't anything personal. He'd made his position clear and she was fine to walk the line he'd drawn.

'Tell me again where Ama's staying?' he asked, folding his arms across his chest.

Olivia tried not to notice the way the scrubs pulled tight against his biceps and to concentrate on what he'd asked, relieved it was all business. They had a brief conversation revolving around Ama's discharge planning and her living arrangements in between ops.

'I'll get Helen to make an appointment for Ama in my rooms on day ten,' he said, making a mental note to tell the very efficient Hunter Clinic senior receptionist when he got back there this afternoon. 'The staples have to come out then, so it might as well be the first follow-up.'

Olivia nodded. 'I'll see that she gets there.'

Ethan studied Olivia for a moment. It sounded as if she wasn't going to be attending herself and he wondered just how much he was going to be seeing of her now. He knew it was a good thing, to get some distance from each other, but perversely he didn't want *not* to see her either.

Talking to her the other day had been harrowing, and he'd been harsh and awful, but he'd felt as if a weight had been lifted from his shoulders.

Hell, he'd slept through three nights in a row.

Olivia turned to go—clearly they were done here. But his 'I need to thank you for the other day,' pulled her up.

She turned and arched an eyebrow.

'I know I was…harsh, and I pushed you away, but…it really helped being able to talk to you… about what happened. About…' he dropped his voice '…Aaliyah. I feel…better. I'm sleeping better.'

Olivia couldn't believe what she was hearing. She shut her eyes against it, wishing it was as easy to shut her ears. She didn't want to know how much *better* Ethan felt. Did he have any clue how much *worse* she felt?

A wave of anger and frustration welled in her at his obliviousness. 'I shouldn't be the only one who knows this, Ethan,' she said, lowering her voice to a scathing whisper as she folded her arms. 'Hell, I can't believe you've never *told* anyone. Don't you think that Leo should at least know?'

Ethan was taken aback by her contemptuous disbelief. He'd never thought to tell Leo. It had all been too big, too horrible even to contemplate. He'd just been hanging on, getting through each day and then Olivia had come back. He and Leo might be closer now, but he doubted they'd ever be *that* close. 'Why?'

Olivia shook her head. 'Dear Lord…why do you *think*, Ethan? Because he's your brother, you idiot. He *loves* you. You've taken all this time to mend your fences and work on your relationship and yet you keep this big…*huge* thing that's been weighing you down and screwing you up for over a year all to yourself? *He's your family*, Ethan, and I know you don't really know how that works, but trust me on this—you share this kind of stuff with each other.'

Ethan frowned. She was really ticked. 'Okay… maybe you're right…maybe it *is* time I told Leo. But I don't understand why you're so angry about it.'

Olivia all but rolled her eyes. *Because I love you too, you idiot.*

'Hey, Olivia, just checking you're—' Kara stopped when she realised that Olivia wasn't alone in the corridor and that things were a little intense between her and Ethan. 'Oh, sorry,' she apologised.

'Don't be,' Olivia said stiffly, glaring at Ethan. 'Perfect timing.'

She turned and gave Kara a strained smile. Kara looked from Olivia to Ethan and then back to Olivia. The look on her face said she wasn't sure at all about the timing.

'You wanted something?' Olivia prompted tersely.

Kara put up her hands in a placatory manner. 'I was just seeing if we were still on to go dress shopping this arvo.'

Olivia groaned inwardly. Damn it. The hospital ball. She'd forgotten that Kara had finally harangued her into going. But with Ama being discharged and spare time on her hands she was going to need something to fill it.

'Sure,' she said, softening her smile and nodding reassuringly at Kara. 'Looking forward to it.' *Like a scalpel to the jugular.*

Kara nodded and scooted away with what Ethan could only describe as indecent haste. 'So…you're going to the ball, then?' he asked.

Ethan had thought she'd resisted all Kara's entreaties to let her hair down and have a night of fun.

Olivia felt tension lock her jaw at the surprise in his voice. Right at this moment she resented the hell out of how well he *thought* he knew her. 'Yes, I am,' she said, her voice not so much of a whisper any more. 'And I'm going to dance with *every* available man there. *And* I will be making it my mission to not go home alone,' she lied. 'You got a problem with that?'

Ethan felt her angry challenge kick him right between the eyes. As it happened, he had *big* problems with it. He knew he had no say over who she did or didn't sleep with, and that she was a free agent, but the thought grabbed at his gut and squeezed hard.

He was aware of the curious gazes of the staff passing by them in the corridor. 'Why don't you say it a little louder?' he said, keeping his tone low.

Olivia saw red. *Patronising bastard.* She opened her mouth to refute his statement about the volume of her voice when a male nurse winked at her as he passed by. 'Put *me* on your dance card, darlin',' he said in a thick Irish accent.

Olivia blinked, startled by the offer, heat flushing her cheeks. 'You got it,' she said, and then smiled as the Irish charmer grinned and clutched his heart, all without missing a step.

Ethan clenched his fists by his sides and made a mental note to talk to the guy about *boundaries.* 'Olivia…' He shook his head. 'This isn't you.'

Olivia returned her gaze to Ethan's face. He did look less tired than she'd seen him. 'Oh, yes it is,' she said testily, lowering her voice again. 'This is who I am now.'

Now he'd made it clear his heart was taken.

Ethan took a step towards her. 'Olivia.'

It was like a punch to his solar plexus when she took a step back, her eyes frosty. It had never been his intention to hurt her. *Again.* He'd laid his cards on the table to *avoid* hurting her. But right now she looked as if she'd never hated him more. Not even that day she'd overheard the argument between him and Leo and called them toxic.

Olivia wanted to step closer so badly she had to grind her feet into the floor to stop herself. Ethan was right—it wasn't her. But she had to break his hold over her.

He was damaged and, damn it, she deserved someone whole.

Someone who had their whole heart to give.

He was waiting for her to say something; she could tell. But there were no words, just a heart that was crumbling in her chest. So she turned and walked away.

There was a knock at Ethan's door at six o'clock the next night. He'd been prowling around his living area non-stop since he'd walked in half an hour ago, and a bottle of whisky was sitting on the kitchen bench.

He felt restless and edgy, but every time he stopped to pour himself a drink he realised he didn't want it. He wished he did—he wished he could drink the whole damn thing and forget about Olivia dancing with every man at the ball.

He didn't know why this was making him so crazy, but he knew whisky wasn't going to make it better.

Right now all he wanted to do was go to Olivia's place, drag her into his arms and kiss her senseless. That was what he craved more than whisky.

But he didn't have the right. He couldn't offer her what she needed. What she deserved.

Leo was standing on his doorstep in a tux when Ethan opened to the second knock. As if he needed another reminder of the ball. 'You really didn't have to dress to come see me,' Ethan said derisively.

'I didn't wear this for *you*, brother dear. My wife usually lasts an hour with me in a tux before she wants me out of it. My motives are purely ulterior.'

Ethan screwed up his face. 'Too much information,' he said, standing aside, indicating for his brother to come in and following Leo's broad shoulders down the short hallway into the living area. 'Did Lizzie send you?'

It had been a clinic day for him today, and Lizzie had been relentless in her campaign to have both Hunter men in tuxes representing the Hunter Clinic at the ball.

'Yes.'

Ethan gave a half laugh, half snort at the bald admission. 'I'm not going to the damn ball.'

Leo folded his arms and didn't look as if he was going to be moving any time soon. Not without Ethan anyway. 'She's going to be annoyed with me if I don't show up with you.'

'Well, only for an hour, by the sounds of it. I'm sure you can tough it out. Flirt with her a little. You might be able to get her out of there in under an hour.'

Leo chuckled and Ethan felt a pang at how obviously happy his brother was to be under the thumb. Ethan watched him stroll towards the kitchen bench, hands in his pockets.

'Good to see you actually have your own whisky instead of always relying on my stash,' he said as he took his hands out and lifted the bottle, inspecting the label. 'You planning on drinking all of this tonight?'

Ethan looked at Leo. He read the unspoken thoughts in his brother's eyes as the spectre of their father rose between them. 'No.' Although a few weeks back he would have given it a good shake.

Leo nodded. He put the bottle down, then perched himself on one of the bar stools. 'Okay. So what's going on with you?' He held up a hand as Ethan started to interrupt. 'I know you and I don't really do this...*talking* stuff...but I do hope you know you *can* talk to me?'

Ethan regarded his brother steadily. He looked uncomfortable, and Ethan knew it couldn't have been easy for Leo to initiate this. They'd had some frank discussions in the last six months. Got a lot of things out in the open. Told some home truths. But those had eventuated from tense, heated conversations. None of them had started out as a simple, *'What's going on with you?'*

And then a thought struck him and he narrowed his eyes. 'Has Olivia been talking to you?' *She wouldn't say anything, surely?*

Leo frowned. 'No.' He looked at his brother speculatively. 'What about?' He sat up straighter. 'Is everything okay?'

Olivia's voice played through Ethan's head.

*'Don't you think that Leo should at least know?'*

*'He's your family, Ethan.'*

*'You share this kind of stuff with each other.'*

'No…she's fine… We had a talk yesterday, that's all. She kind of told me off.'

Leo chuckled. 'She's pretty good at that from what I remember. I don't think anyone can say the word *toxic* with quite as much disgust dripping from it as Olivia.'

Ethan gave a half-smile. She had given them both a right dressing-down that day. 'She reckons I should tell you about what happened to me on tour.'

Leo shook his head. 'I know what happened,

Ethan. The papers gave a pretty good rundown of it and your injuries speak for themselves. I think I can fill in the gaps. I don't want you to rehash it if you don't want to.'

'Not about that,' Ethan said. He headed to the kitchen and grabbed two crystal tumblers from one of the overhead cupboards—this *was* going to require some alcoholic fortification.

He cracked the lid on the bottle of whisky and splashed a couple of fingers in each glass. His hand shook. He couldn't believe he was about to open up to Leo. Prior to three days ago no one had known about Aaliyah, and now not only did Olivia know, he was about to tell Leo also.

But Olivia was right—they were brothers, and if he wanted their relationship to continue, to thrive and grow instead of always being stilted…

And he did want that, he realised.

He pushed a glass towards Leo before swallowing half of his down. 'There was a woman…' he said.

Leo looked at Ethan. 'Oh,' he said, and swallowed half of his whisky down too.

# CHAPTER TWELVE

FOR THE NEXT fifteen minutes Ethan talked and Leo listened. Ethan was grateful for his silence. It enabled him to tell the story of him and Aaliyah in his own words and it all just tumbled out.

'I'm sorry,' Leo said, when Ethan seemed to have talked himself dry.

'Thank you.'

'I wish you'd told me earlier.'

'Yeah,' Ethan acknowledged as he stared into the depths of the whisky he was swirling in his glass. 'Sorry…'

Leo shrugged it off. 'And Olivia knows?'

Ethan nodded grimly. 'She does now.'

'She loves you, you know?'

Ethan glanced up sharply at his brother, pleased he didn't have a mouthful of drink. His heart leapt painfully in his chest at the possibilities. *At the impossibilities.*

'She *told* you that?'

Leo shook his head. 'No. Of course not. But I've seen Olivia in love with you once before, remember? I know what that looks like.'

Ethan shut his eyes. If anybody knew after their love triangle debacle, it was Leo. *This was bad.* He'd seen the other day how her compassion for what he'd been through had melted her heart. Hardly surprising—Olivia always had been one of the most empathetic people he'd ever known. She'd told him ten years ago that his big wounded eyes were what had attracted him to her.

And he'd been aware of the slippery slope. That was why he'd warned her about building castles in the sky.

But if he'd known…if he'd suspected…

*What?* He'd have been more direct? More direct than *I'm damaged goods* and *Steer clear*? The truth was his biggest fear was that he wouldn't have. That he would have ruthlessly taken advantage of her like he had a decade ago. For some reason she'd got back under his skin and he was beginning to crave her more than he'd ever craved whisky.

Ethan shook his head, pushing away the thought, clinging to the memory of the woman he loved. 'I love Aaliyah.'

Leo quirked an eyebrow. 'Are you telling me or yourself?'

Ethan glared at his brother as thunderclouds gathered in his gut. 'I would be very careful what you say next.'

Leo didn't look remotely concerned. 'You think you can only ever love one person, Ethan? Just stop for a moment and think about how *crazy* that is. That means I'd still be hung up on Olivia and have no room for Lizzie.'

Ethan's hand tightened around his glass. The idea of Leo and Olivia clawed at his gut with about the same ferocity as the shame he felt at his actions a decade ago. 'You didn't love Olivia.'

'No. But I could have. If she hadn't been so gung-ho about you.'

Ethan looked down into his drink. 'I'm sorry about that. She really deserved you more than me.'

Leo nodded. 'That's very true.'

Ethan glanced up, startled, then saw the smile

on his brother's face and returned it with a grudging one of his own.

'Look, Ethan, if this Aaliyah was as amazing and compassionate as she sounds do you think she would have wanted you to *never* love again? To never *be* loved? Would you have wanted that for her if, God forbid, it had been you that had stayed behind in the hospital that day?'

Ethan held his brother's gaze, the truth of what he was saying looming large in his brain. Of course Aaliyah wouldn't have wanted that. And nor would he. She'd been a wonderful, passionate, beautiful woman. For her never to have found someone else to share that with would have been a travesty.

'No,' he conceded.

'I think she'd be pretty annoyed about it, don't you?'

Ethan looked into his heart. Aaliyah had been very passionate and opinionated—*annoyed* was probably a mild descriptor.

But still he couldn't let go. 'I can't… I feel like I'm betraying her.'

'Why is it a betrayal?' Leo demanded. 'Loving

again after death and heartache and your whole world going to hell? That's resurrection, Ethan. That's affirmation that the love you felt for Aaliyah wasn't something wasted and lost forever. It honours her memory. It says that loving Aaliyah was so amazing it was worth all the heartache. That love is worth it.'

Ethan's head buzzed at his brother's reasoning.

'And can you look at me—*really* look at me,' Leo said, 'and tell me you don't feel *anything* for Olivia.'

Ethan knew he couldn't do that. His feelings for Olivia had been churning inside him for weeks now, and were becoming more and more muddled since they'd ended up all over each other in his bed. He'd been pushing them away, holding them back, because of the guilt he felt about Aaliyah.

But what if Leo was right? What if there was more than one person for everyone? What if loving again honoured his love for Aaliyah instead of betraying it.

What if he could love Olivia *without* betraying Aaliyah?

'Tell me what you've been feeling since you told Olivia about Aaliyah.'

Ethan dragged in a breath, still trying to wrap his head around the revelations of the night. 'I feel…lighter…better. Like a weight's been lifted. I've carried it around so long it felt like a block around my neck. I've been sleeping so much better. And I haven't had a drop to drink since I told her until now.'

'I think that's called catharsis. Interesting choice of who you chose to tell first, don't you think?'

Ethan shrugged. 'I guess.'

Leo looked at his brother and Ethan felt as if he was being weighed up. 'A little while back you pretty much told me I'd be a fool to let Lizzie out of my life, and so now I'm here, telling you the same thing. I think you love Olivia, but you're too screwed up by your past—not just what happened on tour, but before, way before that, with Mum and Dad—and too frightened of the future to admit it. But make no mistake: you are a fool if you let her get away a second time. Life's short, Ethan. *You* know that more intimately than anyone. Don't blow it by clinging to somebody who you know, deep down, wouldn't ask you for that sacrifice.'

Ethan felt a heat spreading in his chest as possibilities bloomed. Was Leo right? Did he love Olivia? He'd studiously avoided any deep emotional attachment to her last time because his agenda with her had had nothing to do with love.

*But there'd been no agenda this time.*

He tried to push the spreading heat, the possibilities back—he'd really screwed up with Olivia again. 'I think I may have blown any chance with her, Leo.'

'Yeah, knowing you, you've been a complete idiot,' Leo agreed. 'But love forgives, Ethan. Above all, love forgives.'

Leo was looking straight into his eyes and Ethan felt as if his brother wasn't just referring to the situation between him and Olivia. 'You should write for Hallmark,' he joked, because the enormity of what he was contemplating was too, too much.

Leo rolled his eyes. 'Yeah, yeah.'

But then suddenly it seemed right. As if something that had been holding impossibly tight in his gut had just twanged free.

'I love her,' Ethan said, and it came out on such a pent-up rush of emotion he felt as if he'd just breathed his heart up and it was lying on the marble benchtop between them.

He felt panicked and afraid, but also…hopeful.

It took a few moments but Leo smiled at him. Slowly at first, and then bigger, almost in time with the love blooming inside Ethan's chest.

'Well, let's go and get her, then.' Leo grinned, swallowing the dregs of his drink in one hit. 'Come on, Cinderella, you *shall* go to the ball. Where's your tuxedo?'

Olivia had never felt this alone in a room full of people in her life. She could see her reflection in the French doors of the opulent room, and even sipping champagne in a group of people she looked so damn forlorn not even she could bear to look at herself.

Kara had picked out the perfect frock for her—a purple frothy gown with shoestring straps that crisscrossed at her cleavage and spilled down into a full gauzy skirt with thousands of diamantés sewn into it. They shone like stars in the light from the expensive crystal chandeliers. It sat low on her back, making a bra impossible, and brushed against the floor.

She'd twisted her hair up into a hasty knot because she'd been too despondent to wash it, and the only accessories she'd indulged in were a touch of lip gloss and her opal ring.

Kara had exclaimed at how stunning she'd looked when Olivia had made her entrance, and every available man in the room, and a lot of the not so available ones, most certainly agreed. Her dance card was full. Olivia hoped that was just from opportunity rather than from word getting around that she was auditioning men to take home.

She wasn't going home with anyone.

In fact she was counting down the minutes until it might seem respectable enough for her to leave. Alone. When would it be okay to plead a headache and slip out through the door?

She hated that she felt so down. The ballroom was lit by thousands of tiny lights, like a fairy kingdom, and the band that was playing soft melodic jazz would at any other time have delighted her. Hell, the whole room was a visual feast, with the lights and the decorations from something out of *A Midsummer's Night Dream* not to mention the beautiful array of colourful fabrics swirling around.

Gorgeous women sparkled and dashing men dazzled in their elegant tuxedoes. Normally she would have been in her element.

But tonight, despite no shortage of men to dance with, she could barely raise a smile.

Her reflection mocked her. *What did you expect?* And it was right. She shouldn't have expected anything. But a part of her had, deep, *deep* down, hoped that Ethan would swing by and pick her up. That he would gallantly announce that he was her date and the only man she would be going home with.

God! She was such a sucker for a happy ending. And there was nothing like a grand ball to stir that old chestnut.

The man was damaged beyond repair, for crying out loud. And his heart was buried in an ancient arid landscape with a woman she could never compete with.

*Stupid. Stupid. Stupid.*

The lights blurred and formed stars before her eyes as she rapidly blinked back even more stupid tears. This had to stop. She was lucky—things were going well. Ama's surgery had been a success, she and Ril were settled with their host family and Fair Go was thriving.

So many more people in the world had it so much worse—Ama was a classic example of that. She should be deliriously happy.

And she was. But there was an emptiness inside her as well. And there was only one thing that could fill it.

Ethan.

Ethan *freaking* Hunter.

'I do believe you promised me a dance.'

Olivia was dragged from her introspection by a sexy Irish accent. She smiled at the familiar face—a nice-looking man, with kind, flirty eyes.

Far better than dull, lifeless eyes. This man looked as if he knew how to laugh and show a girl a good time.

'I do believe you're right,' she said.

He told her his name was Aidan as he led her to the floor, and when they found some available space he took her in his arms and held her at a comfortable distance. They made some polite chit-chat for a few moments.

'So,' Aidan said. 'You and Ethan, huh?'

Olivia almost tripped over his feet. It was on the tip of her tongue to deny it, but he was so open and honest-looking, so undemanding, she found herself smiling. 'Guilty.'

Aidan sighed dramatically. 'Surgeons get all the hot women. You know, you really should give a male nurse a go. We're *very* good with anatomy and we have a much better bedside manner. Plus—although I can't speak for anyone else—we're always exceedingly grateful.'

Olivia laughed, finally relaxing and enjoying the man's company. 'I'm afraid my heart was a done deal a long time ago.'

'Clearly the man's an A-grade fool.'

Olivia smiled. 'Yes. He's the top of his class.'

'Well, you know, having drunken sex with a lowly male nurse is a great revenge tactic.'

Olivia supposed she should have been shocked or affronted by Aidan's forthright conversation but she wasn't either. His tone was light and his gaze was flirty. She didn't feel threatened or unsafe. Just amused—and God knew she needed a laugh about now.

Aidan was good and kind—it shone from his soul. Not to mention smart—laughing a woman into bed was a very good ploy.

'Thanks. I'll keep it in mind.'

Aidan nodded and they danced for a few moments in silence. 'I'm just saying,' he said, pulling back to look into her face, 'I'd volunteer for the job 'cos that's just the kind of guy I am.'

Olivia laughed. 'You're a trooper. And I appreciate it.'

He sighed again. 'Not going to work, huh?'

Olivia shook her head. 'Sorry. If it's any consolation, I would if…'

Aidan nodded. 'If you weren't head over heels in love with the man who is now pushing his way through a crowded dance floor looking like he wants to make mincemeat of my face.'

Olivia frowned at him. 'What?'

But then an imperious voice, so English compared to the soft burr of Aidan's accent, said, 'May I cut in?'

Aidan looked at a tense-jawed Ethan, then at Olivia. 'It's up to you, darlin',' he said. 'You can dance with him or I can take him outside and beat him up.'

Olivia blinked at Aidan's joviality in the face of what was a fairly hostile situation. Ethan might be dressed in a tux but that was the only civilised thing about him right now as he glared down at the Irishman in stony silence.

'Just say the word,' Aidan chirped.

Olivia did a quick calculation of the body mass difference between the two men and her respect for Aidan trebled. He was going to make some girl an amazing partner one day.

'Thanks.' She smiled at him and squeezed his arm. 'You've been fabulous, but I think I can take it from here.'

Ethan relaxed slightly when the Irish nurse bowed gallantly and melted away. 'May I?' he asked.

Olivia's heart was thrumming against her ribs

so loudly she could barely hear him. 'I didn't think you danced,' she said waspishly.

Ethan grabbed her by the waist and pulled her close. 'I do tonight.'

Olivia's arms went around his neck automatically, for stability, and then just because he looked so damn good and smelled a thousand per cent better. He swayed against her, and for someone who battled a limp and maintained he couldn't dance he managed to get to the end of the song without stepping on her feet or crashing into anyone.

They pulled apart as everyone else did, and clapped politely, but the whole time he was looking at her with lust and heat and sex in his eyes and Olivia's belly turned to mush and her legs to jelly. She felt as if they were the only two people in the room.

'Let's get out of here,' he said as the band started a new song, taking her hand and leading her to the French doors.

By the time they'd stepped out onto a terrace that was lit with enough tiny lights to power an entire fairytale castle Olivia was grateful for the cold air on her heated flesh. Her dress was not suitable for a November night in London, but she was so hot and bothered it was a blessing.

'Ethan, what do you—?'

It was as far as she got before he turned and cut her off with a kiss that was so deep and hard and hungry all she could do was shut her eyes and hang on.

When he pulled away they were both panting, and Olivia was annoyed at herself for being swept away by the lights and the dancing and his dashing frame filling out a tuxedo as well as he did a pair of scrubs.

Hell, the man had even shaved.

'What do you think you're doing?' she demanded.

Ethan had been rehearsing his speech on the way over in a taxi with Leo, but then he'd seen her dancing with Irish and it had wiped everything other than the urge to break fingers from his brain. And then he'd been holding her, and she looked so damn good and so incredibly sexy there was no way he was ever going to remember the impassioned entreaty he'd worked on with Leo.

'I've been incredibly stupid,' he said.

Olivia blinked. 'You have?'

Ethan nodded. 'Yes. I have. I love you. I'm in love with you. But I couldn't admit it to myself. I felt bad even feeling it, and then Leo said—'

'Leo?' Olivia interrupted as her heart started to beat a little bit faster at the possibilities he was presenting.

'Yes, he came over and we talked, and I told him about Aaliyah, and he made me see that she would never have wanted me to bury my heart and my life with her.'

'Oh,' she said faintly, noting the bright glow in his eyes as the golden flecks outshone the fairy lights. Did this mean what she thought it meant? Dared she hope? Her pulse tripped at the thought.

Ethan pushed his fingers into her hair, cradling her cheeks, itching to pull it out of the knot and see it cascade down her shoulders, feel the heavy warmth of it sifting over his fingers.

'I've just been so…lost, Olivia. After Aaliyah I felt like I'd lost *everything*, and I was just existing in this dark, cold, barren place. And then you came back and brought the warmth and the light, and you got under my skin, just like you had the first time, and I tried to ignore that, tried to not want it, but I couldn't.'

Olivia fought against the urge to throw herself into his arms. She wanted him to be sure. 'Because you love me?'

Ethan nodded. 'Yes. You were right when you said Aaliyah wouldn't want me to blame myself for her death, and Leo was right about how Aaliyah would want me to love and *be loved* again. I guess I needed to open up to the people who love me and let them help me through, because when I did…it suddenly made sense. But you know us Hunters—not big on emotional declarations.'

Olivia could feel a block of emotion rising in her throat. Why hadn't the stubborn man had this kind of revelation a bit earlier? 'Oh, Ethan.'

Ethan was encouraged by the husky quality of her voice. 'I know I don't deserve a second chance. That all I ever seem to do is hurt you, Liv. But—'

Olivia cut him off with her mouth, raising herself up on her tippy-toes and throwing her arms around his neck. She didn't care about that.

There'd been a decade of hurt between them, but he loved her and they had a lot of decades ahead.

'Yes, you do,' she said, pulling back after long breathless moments. 'We both do. So we screwed it up in the past? This is now, and we *both* deserve this. We're good people who have had crappy things happen to them—you bet your ass we deserve this. And you'd better be in this forever, Ethan Hunter, because I love you too, and *together forever* is the only second chance I'm interested in.'

Ethan smiled, and then he laughed, lifting her off her feet and swirling her around and around, her diamantés dazzling and sparkling. He felt as light as the air he was swirling her in, and more alive than he'd been in a very long time.

He eased her back to the floor and placed his forehead against hers. 'For ever and ever, Liv, I promise.'

And then he kissed her. He kissed her with everything he had, showing her all their tomorrows.

And it was good.

# EPILOGUE

IT HAD BEEN a perfect day for a wedding. Not even a frosty October day had stopped the bride from wearing her mother's immaculately restored wedding dress. The vintage piece from 1950 fell only to the knee, and the cap sleeves bared her arms, but inside the opulent function room of one of London's swankiest hotels it was warm and cosy.

The tinkling of glasses caused a hush around the room and the occupants all turned to face the bridal table, draped in filmy white and decorated with sprigs of fluffy yellow wattle to match the touches of the Australian wild flower in the bride's hair and bouquet.

Leo Hunter stood up in his place and announced, 'It's been a hell of a year.'

A murmur of agreement ran around the wedding guests. Some laughed. Everyone smiled.

Lizzie especially, who slipped her free hand into her husband's and squeezed. In her other she cradled their sleeping three-month-old baby girl. Little Francesca was the spitting image of her father and the light of their lives.

'It took a decade to get these two—' he turned to Ethan, sitting beside him, and Olivia, sitting on the other side of her new husband '—together, and another year for them to finally tie the knot amidst their busy schedules, but I think we can all agree it's been worth the wait.'

More general agreement and smiles.

'I'm not going to go on. I think everyone here knows that the Hunter men aren't big on all that mushy, emotional stuff.'

General laughter now at the understatement. Everyone present knew the Hunter siblings were great at terse exchanges and loaded silences and only reasonably new to the whole brotherly love thing.

'I just wish Ethan and Olivia all the love and happiness I know they both deserve. I also wish them luck in their new endeavour as they set off to Africa to train up local teams at the new facility the Hunter Clinic and Fair Go have jointly funded.' Leo raised his glass and turned slightly to face the bride and groom. 'To Ethan and Olivia. Good things always.'

Ethan and Olivia rose from their seats as people toasted them. Ethan held his hand out to Leo and they shook. 'Thank you,' he murmured as myriad glasses clinked together. 'It means a lot to me to have you by my side today.'

Olivia watched as Ethan and Leo embraced, tears pricking the backs of her eyes. She looked at Lizzie, who smiled and winked at her through suspiciously bright eyes.

Ethan waited for his brother to take his seat, clearing his throat from a rush of unexpected emotion, then turned to Olivia, who was glowing for more reasons than one. A surge of pure male pride flooded him at knowing that *he* was responsible for that look on her face, that *he* was the one going home with her tonight and every night.

He squeezed her hand as he turned to address the room and said, 'I think we can all agree that I'm the luckiest man in this room tonight.' Then he turned back to Olivia, dipped his head and kissed her very thoroughly to a resounding chorus of applause, cheers and hoots.

When he finally released her it was gratifying to see the way her dark brown eyes had melted into two thick, sludgy pools of sticky-sweet lust more desirous than any chocolate from Sirmontane.

Collecting himself from his own libido spike, he turned to speak again.

'As Leo said, we're not known for our emotional monologues, so I'm going to keep this brief too. I'd like to thank everyone for coming and helping us to celebrate our day. It *has* been a hell of a year, and it's great to look out at you all and see how many of us from the Hunter Clinic family have found happiness in that time. There must be something in the water.'

Everyone laughed and he waited for them to quiet down before he continued.

'For a long time I'd resigned myself to not ever being happy. Truly happy. And then along came Olivia…again…and she has made me happier than I ever knew I could be.'

He looked down at her and smiled as the room filled with coos and wolf-whistles.

Ethan faced their guests again. 'Up until last night I didn't think it could get any better than this—which just goes to prove you *can* get to thirty-six and know nothing, because now it appears I'm going to be a daddy and I'm no longer *just* happy, I'm whole.'

For a moment there was stunned silence, and then the room erupted in wild applause as the grinning parents-to-be were treated to a standing ovation.

'And now, if no one objects,' Ethan said as he hushed their guests with a raising of his hands, 'I'm going to dance with my pregnant wife.'

Hoots and hollers met his proclamation as he took Olivia's hand and gestured for her to accompany him.

Olivia looked at her brand-new tuxedoed husband. 'We don't have to dance, Ethan,' she said over the din.

Ethan smiled. 'Yes, we do. I've been taking lessons.'

'Lessons?'

'Trust me,' he said, kissing her again. 'I'm a doctor.'

But their path to the dance floor was littered with well-wishers and it was a slow trip.

Lizzie and Leo were the first to embrace them.

'Welcome to the club, Ethan,' Leo said, and both Lizzie and Olivia were surprised when the brothers embraced again.

Iain and Lexi were next in line. Little Bonnie, recently adopted from China, was alert in her father's arms and smiled at the newlyweds in a way that melted Olivia's heart.

'She's such a cutie,' Olivia said.

Lexi smiled. 'Just like her father.'

Kara and Declan stopped them next, Kara giving Olivia a huge hug. They were both brown and relaxed, having not long returned from their honeymoon on the Great Barrier Reef.

'You know I'm taking total credit for this, right?' Kara said. 'If I hadn't badgered you to go to the ball...'

Ethan laughed. 'Okay, you can take the credit for the wedding, but *I'm* taking credit for the baby.'

Declan laughed. 'I'm sure Kara will give you that one.'

Marco and Becca were the last ones to catch them before they got to the dance floor.

'Zorro,' Ethan said, offering his hand to the other man, not remotely concerned to be addressing the second in line to the royal throne of Sirmontane so casually. 'So glad you could come and add a touch of royalty to our humble wedding. Not quite as spectacular as *your* marvellous celebration last year.'

Marco grinned at the familiar jovial banter. 'Nowhere near as many people to potentially offend either,' he said good-naturedly. 'Weddings, my friend, are just the icing. The cake,' he said, smiling down at Becca, 'is always the best bit.'

Becca rolled her eyes and clutched playfully at her heart. 'Such poetry, my darling.'

'Are you going to be okay, Clavo, with your limp and your two left feet?' Marco teased. 'If you need me to do the honours...?'

Marco, known for his ability to tango, had been Ethan's go-to man when he'd considered taking some dance lessons so he could wow Olivia in their first dance as husband and wife. The royal Prince and fellow war veteran had set him up with some exclusive lessons from a friend who ran a Latin dance club in Soho.

'You take care of your own wife.' Ethan winked. 'I'll take care of mine.'

And with that Olivia was finally alone with her husband on the dance floor. The strains of something soft and sweet filled the room as he swept her along in a dance that was slow and simple and sexy and all she had to do was follow his lead.

They didn't talk, because clearly the world's most competent surgeon was concentrating too hard on not screwing up, but Olivia's heart almost exploded in her chest at his willingness to go so far out of his comfort zone for her.

His limp was barely discernible these days, due to his strict adherence to regular physio—something which he demonstrated ably as the song came to an end and he dipped her dramatically, following through with a searing kiss to cat-calls, applause and wolf-whistles.

Another song struck up as Ethan righted

Olivia and other couples joined them on the dance floor. Ethan moved into a slow shuffle. The scent of wattle and happiness suffused his senses as he pulled her closer.

'You look very sexy, Mrs Hunter,' Ethan murmured in Olivia's ear, even though he knew his independent wife was not changing her name.

'You're not bad yourself, Mr Hunter,' she murmured. 'Of course scrubs would have worked just as well for me.'

Ethan chuckled. 'I have some in the hotel suite.'

Olivia pulled her head off his shoulder swiftly, looking up at him. His cheeky grin let her know he was teasing. She shook her head at him.

'Oh, look, Ethan,' she murmured as the cutest sight caught her attention over his shoulder.

She danced them around slightly so they could both witness it. Their two flower girls were dancing with the page boy, holding hands in a circle. Mia, the eldest, was six and was Mitch Cooper's daughter. As they watched Mitch and Grace cut in. Mitch picked up Mia and all three of them danced together, their arms around each other. Olivia even heard Mia call Grace *Mummy* and her heart swelled in her chest. She knew how much Grace had wanted to hear that word from the little girl she loved like her own.

That just left Ella and Isaac dancing together. At two and a half, Ella looked the picture of health after her risky experimental cancer treatment in the US over a year ago had been more than successful.

Olivia glanced over at Rafael and Abbie, whose marriage had almost disintegrated under the strain of their daughter's illness. They were watching Ella like the two proudest people on earth, and their four-month-old son, Stefano, with dark curls just like his sister's, was proof that things were very good between them.

Isaac, who was five, was dancing with Ella a bit like the way Ethan had danced with her, his little tongue stuck out in concentration as if he was trying to be all grown up and not step on her toes. Olivia located Charlotte and Edward up amongst the band. She'd hired the band on Edward's recommendation and watching him now, seated at the baby grand piano, his fingers tinkling the ivories, she was glad she had. Edward was obviously familiar with the guys and they were happy to have him up with them, playing the piano like a professional musician instead of a microsurgeon.

Charlotte was sitting beside him, enjoying the show, but Olivia noticed her glancing frequently over at Isaac, keeping a watchful eye on him. As a single mum to Isaac for so long, Olivia knew that Charlotte found it hard not to hover, but Edward's love and commitment had made her more secure. Charlotte looked blissfully happy. They both did.

*Seemed it was the night for it.*

'How long do you think,' Ethan asked, nuzzling her neck, bringing her attention back to the tight circle between them and the heat that was building with every rock and sway, 'until we can leave?'

Olivia smiled into his shoulder. 'Well, I *am* pregnant. And pregnant women *do* get very tired.'

Ethan grinned, his lips just below her ear. 'I like the way you think.'

'Good,' she said. 'Give me your jacket and get me out of here.'

Ethan grabbed her hand and pushed her out into a twirl before pulling her back in and dipping her.

'Yes, ma'am,' he muttered against her mouth.

* * * * *